## *THE BOBBSEY TWINS*
### AND THEIR CAMEL ADVENTURE

No matter where they go, the Bobbsey twins are bound to run into mystery and excitement, and Egypt is no exception. Actually, the camel adventure starts in Italy where the Bobbseys, their friends, Nellie Parks and Charlie Mason, and—yes, their old enemy Danny Rugg, have arrived in Venice.

Mr. Abdel Gouda, a wealthy Egyptian gentleman, has a priceless little antique horse to donate to the Lakeport Museum if the children and the leaders of their European tour will come to Cairo to receive it.

Scarcely have the Bobbseys reached Mr. Gouda's home when things begin to happen. Salah, a trusted servant sent to fetch the horse, disappears and with him the valuable antique. Farah, the trained racing camel, is stolen from her little Egyptian master, ten-year-old Ali. Here are not one but two challenges for the Bobbsey twins!

How they solve the double mystery in the shadow of the pyramids and at the same time get into all the mischief four lively children can dream up is a hilarious story younger readers will love.

# THE BOBBSEY TWINS BOOKS
## By Laura Lee Hope

---

The mysterious figure heard the splash!

# The Bobbsey Twins and Their Camel Adventure

*By*

LAURA LEE HOPE

GROSSET & DUNLAP
*Publishers*     *New York*

# CONTENTS

# Content

# CHAPTER I

## AN EXCITING INVITATION

"LOOK! That boy on shore is calling us!" Blond Flossie Bobbsey pointed from the Italian gondola on the Grand Canal in Venice, Italy.

Her six-year-old twin Freddie looked across the rippling water. "We'd better see what he wants."

Their brother and sister Bert and Nan Bobbsey, who were twelve and twins also, agreed. Nellie Parks and Charlie Mason, who were with them, nodded. But the fourth American boy in the boat, Danny Rugg, whined, "Aw, do we have to go in?"

All of the children lived in Lakeport, U. S. A., and were on a tour which had been arranged by a summer camp. In charge of the tour were Tom Thompson, twenty-two, and his sister Terry, twenty, popular camp counselors. Tom called to the gondolier to make a landing at one of the bright red-and-white striped poles. He wore a flat straw hat with a tiny red ribbon band.

1

"It's Mario, the bellboy from the hotel!" Bert exclaimed. "I wonder what he wants. He looks excited."

In a few minutes the children stepped ashore onto the marble paving of St. Mark's Square and looked at Mario. The bellboy was about ten, with dark curly hair. His brown eyes shone as he announced, "The American consul, Signor Baxter, is at the hotel, Signor Thompson. He asks to see you at once!"

"What does he want?" Nan Bobbsey inquired.

Mario shrugged and led the way out of the huge square and down a narrow street.

"It's very mysterious!" Flossie said as she skipped along by Nellie's side.

The pretty blond girl smiled at Flossie. "You Bobbseys seem to find mysteries wherever you go!"

Charlie Mason overheard her. "You're right! And I'd be willing to bet they'll run into one on this trip too!"

"I hope so," Nan declared. "We had lots of fun in our SEARCH FOR THE GREEN ROOSTER in Portugal."

The Bobbsey twins loved mysteries and had solved many. In THE GREEK HAT MYSTERY they had helped to capture some thieves who were smuggling Greek statues out of the country. Earlier, in THE BIG RIVER MYS-

TERY, they had recovered two family heirlooms from the Hudson River.

As Tom and the children trooped into the hotel lobby a tall, slender man got up from a chair and came toward them. "Mr. Thompson?" he asked in a deep voice.

When Tom nodded, the consul said, "May I see you alone? I have an important matter to discuss with you."

"Certainly," the young counselor replied. After telling the children that they might return to the square, he led the government official into a small writing room.

"What do you suppose that's all about?" Bert wondered.

"Perhaps," said Nan, "it's about us going home sooner."

"Come on!" Freddie urged. "I want to see those pigeons again!"

The Bobbseys, Nellie, Charlie, and Danny made their way back to the principal square of Venice. Arcades ran along three sides. The fourth side was occupied by an ornate church.

"All the pigeons in the world must be here!" Flossie declared as they walked toward the center of the large open space.

Thousands of the birds strutted over the paving or flew onto the shoulders of strolling tourists. Suddenly a pigeon lighted on Flossie's blond curls. "Take my picture, Freddie!" she squealed in delight.

Her twin focused his little camera. "Hold still!" he cautioned.

At the same moment Danny Rugg pulled a slingshot from his pocket. Carefully he took aim at the pigeon on Flossie's head.

"Stop that!" Bert leaped on Danny and tore the slingshot from his hand. The two boys tumbled to the ground and began to tussle.

"Bert! Danny!" Nan cried out. "Get up!"

Shamefaced, the two struggled to their feet. "I wasn't going to hit Flossie!" Danny protested indignantly. "I just wanted to scare the pigeon!"

"Let's go back to the hotel," Nellie proposed. "Maybe we can find out what Mr. Baxter wanted with Tom."

Freddie and Flossie had wandered away to buy corn from a peddler to feed the pigeons. They ran back when Nan called to them.

"The birds ate right out of my hand!" Flossie said proudly.

Tom, tall and muscular, was waiting in the lobby when the Lakeport children reached the hotel. "Come out onto the terrace," he urged. "I have something important to tell all the members of the tour."

Terry Thompson, a pretty, athletic-looking girl, was waiting on the balcony with the other two tour leaders and eight more children. They

"Take my picture, Freddie!" Flossie squealed in delight

had just returned from a sightseeing trip to one of the neighboring islands and were laden with souvenirs.

"I have a very interesting invitation for you," Tom began when they were all settled. "How many of you would like to go to Egypt?"

Noticing the bewildered expressions on the children's faces, the young man explained that a Mr. Gouda, a wealthy gentleman who lived in Cairo, had become interested in the Lakeport Museum. "He would like to donate an extremely valuable antique to the children's section of our museum at home. It's a toy horse," Tom told them.

"What does it look like?" Freddie asked eagerly.

"Can I ride it?" Flossie interrupted.

"Wait a minute. Hold your horses. I mean—" Tom caught himself.

The children giggled.

"I don't know too much about the toy horse yet. But I do know that it's very valuable. It seems the officer in our consular office in Cairo was supposed to deliver the toy horse to Lakeport. But he has since been transferred to another post and will not be going back to the United States."

"Then the museum won't get the toy horse?" Nan asked, somewhat disappointed.

Tom grinned. "My uncle, who's now the consular officer in Cairo, knew that Terry and I were to be in Venice. He suggested that we take the horse back to America."

"Then you're going to Egypt?" Nan asked.

Tom nodded. "*And* any of you children who want to join Terry and me in this adventure. Mr. Gouda has offered to pay the expenses, and you can stay in his house in Cairo. Would anyone like to go?"

"What's in Cairo?" Flossie asked.

"Oh, there are pyramids that almost reach the sky, they're so high. One pyramid has over four hundred steps! There's a sphinx, too, which has the head of a king and the body of a lion!"

"Could we ride a camel?" Bert put in.

"Sure enough."

One of the other children asked, "What will we do if we don't go there?"

"The rest of you will go on with the other counselors to Switzerland."

"Oh, I want to see the Sph-ph-phinx!" Flossie exclaimed.

"So do I!" said Freddie. "And buy a camel to take home." Everyone laughed.

A babble of voices broke out as the children tried to decide which of the trips to take. In the end the four Bobbseys and Danny voted to go to Egypt.

Tom stood up. "Okay," he said, "I'll cable your parents for permission. As soon as I get replies we'll make plane reservations for Cairo."

"Ooh, Nan!" Flossie breathed. "I hope Mommy and Daddy answer soon!"

After lunch and a short rest the group set out for more sightseeing in St. Mark's Square. This time Terry came too. "Look at that beautiful church!" Nellie whispered to Nan. There were gold statues all along the roof.

*Clang! Clang! Clang!*

Spellbound, the children watched two bronze figures strike the hour of three on a huge bell atop a tower near the cathedral. As the sound of the three clangs died away, two bronze figures on the other side of the bell raised their hammers.

*Clang! Clang! Clang!*

"They've already struck the hour," Danny remarked in a disgusted tone. "That's a crazy clock!"

The children's Italian guide smiled. "They always strike twice for the people who didn't listen the first time!"

The guide told the children that Venice was slowly sinking into the sea. "At high tide the water sometimes covers the square and the floor of the church."

The group was led into the Doges' Palace nearby. The guide said that the ancient governors of the city had been called Doges and had lived in this huge building.

He took them across a courtyard and up a long

flight of stone steps, then down a corridor which overlooked the court on one side. Standing on the other side were statues and stone figures.

Tom stopped before a carved lion's head set into the wall. Its mouth was open. "This is a mean-looking animal," he declared.

"That is a very special lion," the guide said. "In the time of the Doges it was used by Venetian citizens to bring their enemies to trial."

"How did they do that?" Danny asked. He walked over and peered curiously at the lion head.

The children gathered around as the man told them, "When a Venetian citizen suspected another man or even if he only had a grudge against him, he would write the man's name on a slip of paper and drop it into the lion's mouth. The names were collected and the men whose names were on the papers were brought before the judges."

"And they never knew who put their names in the lion's mouth?" Bert asked.

The guide shook his head.

"That doesn't seem fair!" Nan spoke up indignantly. The others agreed.

The group of children followed the guide from room to room of the huge building. As they strolled along the corridor, Flossie suddenly stopped.

"Oh, look!" she cried, pointing upward to the

high, domed ceiling. On it were painted many delicately colored figures.

They continued on and entered a wood-paneled room. In one corner was a raised platform with a large, elaborately carved chair on it.

"This is the Hall of Justice where the trials were held," the guide noted. "And that platform is where the chief magistrate presided."

Freddie eagerly ran toward the oversized chair and climbed up.

"Silly," Flossie said, giggling. "You don't look like a judge."

The young visitors wandered around the old room, trying to imagine it as it had been hundreds of years before.

The guide pointed out an opening in the dark wall. "The papers with the names on them landed here when they were dropped into the lion's mouth."

Flossie lingered behind as the others went on. Standing on tiptoe, she gingerly put her hand into the hole. An astonished expression came over her face.

"There's a paper in here!" Flossie cried.

# CHAPTER II

## A TRICK

"A PAPER?" Bert exclaimed, running toward his little sister. "Let's see it!"

"Quick! Open it!" Nan urged.

The others watched breathlessly as Bert unfolded the paper. He looked startled, then a strange expression came over his face.

"It—it says I'm bad!" Bert read the message. " 'Bert Bobbsey is a traitor! He should be run out of Venice!' "

There was a moment of surprised silence, then Nan grabbed the paper from her twin's hand. "Let me see that!" she cried indignantly.

The others watched while Nan studied the note. After a few moments she looked straight at Danny Rugg. "This is your writing!" she accused him.

"Who says so?" Danny sputtered. When he saw the other children's disgusted expressions, he grumbled, "I just thought I'd give Bert a scare!"

"Good joke," Bert said with a grin, "but watch out!"

The guide led the group from the building, then said good-by. The children followed Tom and Terry across the square and down the narrow street toward their hotel. Danny was up in front with one of the other boys. The older Bobbsey twins brought up the rear with Nellie and Charlie.

"Count on Danny to play a trick on you, Bert!" Charlie remarked.

"It wasn't so bad as most of his are," Bert replied. "He's been pretty good on this trip."

"He loves tricks so much, why don't we play one on him?" Nellie suggested.

"That's a good idea," Nan agreed. "Let's think of something!"

The four children were silent several seconds, then Nan smiled broadly.

"Thought of something, Sis?" Bert asked.

Nan nodded. "You know how much Danny likes spaghetti and how little he likes kittens. Well, how about this?" She told them her plan.

"That's great!" Charlie cried.

"How will we manage it?" Nellie asked.

"Alfredo! You know, the waiter at our table," Bert spoke up. "I'll bet he'd help us!"

When they reached the hotel, Bert and Charlie made their way to the kitchen while Nan and Nellie waited in the lounge. In a few minutes the boys returned.

"What did Alfredo say?" Nan said eagerly.

Bert made a victory sign with his fingers. "He'll do it!"

The girls giggled. "I can hardly wait to see Danny's face!" Nellie said.

The boys hurried off on their errand while the girls went upstairs to get ready for dinner. An hour later the whole group met in the hotel dining room.

Bert nodded in reply to the girls' looks of inquiry. Tom and Terry sat at the table with the Lakeport children.

"I'm hungry!" Danny announced as the soup was served. "I hope we have some of that good spaghetti!"

Before they had started to eat, Alfredo hurried back to the table. "'Scuse please." The waiter picked up Danny's bowl of soup just as the boy lifted his spoon.

Nan gulped and hastily covered her smirk with her napkin.

"What's going on? Bring my soup back!" Danny demanded.

Bert said, "Alfredo probably just wants to make sure it is good enough for you."

Danny frowned. Then, thinking he was receiving special treatment, he sat back to wait for his delicious soup.

"Well, where is it?" Danny asked after a few minutes.

The children looked at one another, trying not to laugh. Terry and Tom wondered what new trick the Bobbseys were up to. Presently Alfredo returned with plates piled high with spaghetti.

"Where is my soup?" Danny asked the hurrying waiter.

"Oh, no good, no good! Try this delicious spaghetti!" Alfredo said, while clearing off the other soup dishes.

Everyone began to eat the slippery Italian spaghetti. Danny dug into his portion hungrily.

Nan giggled when she saw Alfredo rushing toward their table again. " 'Scuse please again," he said and picked up Danny's plate. The boy's mouth dropped open as he watched his spaghetti dinner disappear behind the kitchen door.

"What's the matter with that guy?" Danny asked, furious. "I'm going to find out what Alfredo did with my dinner!" The indignant boy marched toward the kitchen.

When all the children started to follow him, Tom asked Terry, "Now what do *you* think they've done?"

"Beats me." His sister shrugged. "Let's go find out."

When the two counselors walked into the

" 'Scuse please again," the waiter said

kitchen, Alfredo was grinning and all the children were laughing with delight except Danny. He was glowering at the sight of five kittens lapping up his soup and spaghetti!

"Oh, aren't they precious!" Terry exclaimed, picking up one of the well-fed kittens.

Bert spoke up. "It was just a joke, Danny. Cheer up! Alfredo has prepared another dinner for you, with double helpings of everything!"

At that Danny managed a smile but muttered as they left the kitchen, "Fat cats!"

The next morning when the tour group gathered in the lobby to learn the day's program, Nan said to Bert, "I wish we'd hear from Mother and Daddy about our trip to Egypt. It would be terrible if they wouldn't let us go."

Bert looked gloomy at the idea. "Tom's at the desk now," he said. "Maybe he has some news."

The counselor came toward the Bobbseys, a broad grin on his face. "Back upstairs, you Bobbseys and Danny. Pack your things. You're going to Egypt!"

"Hurrah!" cried Freddie.

Tom told them that he had received cables from their parents, giving permission to make the trip to Cairo. "I've checked with the airport. We can get a plane at eleven, but we'll have to hurry!"

The Bobbseys and Danny quickly said good-by to the other children and ran toward the elevator.

"I'm sure glad I brought my fire engine," Freddie told Bert as he put the toy in his suitcase. "There might be a fire in Egypt."

Ever since he was a small boy Freddie had loved fire engines and planned to be a fireman when he grew up.

As soon as the packing was finished, the Egypt-bound group hurried to the airport and boarded the plane. They had lunch high over the blue Mediterranean Sea and landed in Cairo during the early afternoon.

"This country is awful flat!" Flossie observed as they drove toward the city. Nothing but great stretches of sand could be seen in every direction.

"And there isn't any grass!" Freddie complained.

Tom told the children that most of Egypt was desert. "It's only along the Nile River that you will see crops growing."

By this time the car had entered the city of Cairo. After a drive along a wide street bordered by palm trees, they drew up before an imposing stone house surrounded by a large garden. A tall, portly man with gray hair hurried out to meet them. He wore a brown-checkered, short-sleeved shirt and Bermuda shorts. "I am Abdel Gouda," he said. "I welcome you to my house."

Tom, Terry, and the five children shook hands with their host. "I hope you will call me Uncle Abdel while you are here," he said. "I have many young friends and that is what they all call me."

Flossie put her hand in Mr. Gouda's and looked up at him. "We'll be your friends too, Uncle Abdel," she assured him.

"And this is my chief servant. His name is Salah and he will look after you while you are here." Mr. Gouda introduced a tall, thin man with a dark complexion and a wisp of a mustache. He wore a long gown of blue and white striped cotton, and a white turban was wound around his head. He bowed solemnly to the children.

"You will find that most Egyptians speak English as well as Arabic," their host assured his guests.

"This way, please," Salah said with a smile and led the group up a wide marble stairway to their rooms.

A short time later they came downstairs to find Uncle Abdel waiting for them in his study. "I think the first place you should visit in Cairo," he told the group, "is the Egyptian Museum. There you will see most of the treasures of ancient Egypt."

"May we see the toy horse, please?" Flossie piped up.

"Ah, yes. I have sent Salah to get it. You see, I purchased it from my archaeologist friend, Mr. Mallakh. He has been keeping it for me until your arrival. By the time we return from the museum, Salah will be back with the horse."

Two long, sleek cars stood at the curb as the group left the house. Mr. Gouda explained that his chauffeur would drive one and he would take the other. "We are too many for one car."

The visitors were fascinated by the crowds on the streets.

"Why do some of the people wear long nightgowns?" Flossie spoke up, her blond curls blowing in the hot breeze. "And look at that lady with the ring in her nose!"

Uncle Abdel informed Freddie and Flossie, "Those nightgowns are called *caftans*. You have probably noticed that many of the Egyptian men wear white turbans. Some have bright red or dark blue ones. The lady with the ring in her nose probably belongs to one of the tribes that wander in caravans through the desert."

"Look!" Flossie cried. "The boy over there is wearing his pajamas!"

"Many of our children wear such suits," Uncle Abdel told her. "They're really cooler than the type of clothes you wear."

Freddie pointed to a passing bus. "There are a whole lot of children singing. They've got their pajamas on too."

"I think the bus is from the mission school near the desert. Some of those children are orphans," Uncle Abdel said.

"You mean a lot of them don't have any Mommies and Daddies!" Flossie spoke up.

"That's right," Terry declared.

Uncle Abdel went on. "But the mission takes good care of them. The children usually have special trips once a week to all kinds of places. One week, I believe, some forty of them took camels out to the pyramids."

"Gee, I wish our school were out here!" Freddie said. "I'd like to go to school on a camel!"

The cars turned into a large square with a park in the center and pulled up before a building of light-colored stone. As the group walked toward the entrance, Mr. Gouda pointed to a small pool. "Those lily-like flowers floating in the water are called lotus, and the plants growing in the center are papyri. The ancient Egyptians made paper from them."

Inside the museum Uncle Abdel led the group up to the second floor where the treasures which had been found in King Tutankhamen's tomb were displayed.

"The king died when he was only eighteen years old, and all his treasures were buried with him!" Uncle Abdel told the children.

"Only a teen-ager when he ruled Egypt!" Danny exclaimed.

The children marveled at the array of royal clothing, weapons, furniture, and jewelry.

"How did the Egyptians ever manage to sit in that chair?" Nan inquired, pointing to a wooden chair that was raised only a few inches from the floor.

"The Egyptians liked to sit on low chairs with their feet tucked under them," Mr. Gouda answered.

"They even have a display of the king's games!" Nan said delightedly.

"That looks like dominoes!" Danny pointed to an ivory box with carved pieces arranged in it.

"That is the ancient game of senet," said Uncle Abdel. "I have an antique reproduction at home, if you would like to learn how to play it!"

"Oh, yes!" The other children were eager to learn senet also.

"And see the jewelry!" Nan exclaimed, bending over a case filled with necklaces, bracelets, and pins of intricately worked gold.

Uncle Abdel looked at his watch. "I'm afraid we must go now," he said. "You will want to come back to the museum many, many times before you leave Cairo. It is impossible to see everything in one visit."

In the lower hall a distinguished-looking man called to Uncle Abdel. "I must talk to him," Mr. Gouda told the children. "I will meet you in the car."

The children stopped to look at one of the tall statues.

"What a beautiful gold headdress she is wearing!" Terry commented.

"It has an awful lot of tiny gold pinwheels in it!" Danny noted.

Nan had walked ahead of the others. As she neared the entrance door of the museum she heard scurrying footsteps behind her. Nan turned to see if it were one of the other children. Instead, she saw a tall Egyptian with a short white beard. He wore a long, dark green caftan and a brown turban. Something was shining on his forefinger. As he hurriedly approached the entrance, Nan glimpsed on his left forefinger a gold ring set with a large black stone.

Not stopping to look left or right, he hurried toward Nan. The next second he accidentally knocked her hard against the wall!

# CHAPTER III

## STREET FIRE!

"OH!" Nan gasped as she struggled to keep from falling. The bearded man was in such a hurry that he did not even stop to help her.

Bert hurried up to his sister. "What happened? I thought I saw someone bump into you!"

"You did. I don't think he even saw me!"

"Well," said Bert hotly, "I'm going to find him and make him apologize to you! What did he look like?"

Nan described the rude Egyptian, then added, "He wore a beautiful ring. I think it had a black scarab stone in it." She remembered from a history lesson that Egyptians use designs of beetles called scarabs.

Bert rushed out the door to track down the white-bearded man. In a few seconds he returned, a puzzled look on his face.

"Did you see him?" Nan asked.

"Yes," Bert replied, "but I couldn't catch him. He got into a taxi with another Egyptian. And Nan, the other man looked like Uncle Abdel's servant, Salah!"

"What would he be doing here?" Nan asked. "He went to Mr. Mallakh's to pick up the toy horse."

"I know," Bert agreed. "It couldn't have been Salah, but this man wore the same kind of blue and white striped robe."

Bert and Nan decided not to say anything to Uncle Abdel about the incident and followed the others out to the cars.

It was late afternoon when they reached the house. Not far away, workmen were swarming over a large vacant lot.

Noticing the children's interest, Mr. Gouda said, "They are getting ready to put up an apartment house."

"May I go down and watch?" Freddie asked as the others went into the house.

"Yes, but don't stay long."

"I'll be back in a few minutes," Freddie replied.

He walked toward the lot. Most of the workmen wore long caftans made of bright blue and white cloth. Some of the men had tucked their robes up around their waists. They were working busily with picks and shovels. The little boy watched intently as the men went about their task.

When Freddie turned to go home, he noticed a small fire in the gutter. A pile of twigs was burning fiercely.

"A fire!" cried Freddie. "I'll get my engine and put it out before it spreads any farther! It's a good thing I filled the tank!"

The little boy dashed back to the house and up to his room. He hastily grabbed the toy engine and raced back to the street. The next second he was directing a stream of water on the little fire. It sizzled and went out.

"Eeeh! Stop!"

Freddie turned at the sound. A man in a dirty, ragged caftan was running toward the little boy, shaking his fist and yelling.

Freddie stood still, too frightened to say anything. At that moment a servant hurried from Uncle Abdel's house. He grabbed the ragged man, who flung his arms around and spoke angrily in Arabic.

Finally he stopped, and the servant smiled. He turned to Freddie. "The man says you put out the fire he had built to cook his *foule!*"

"He was going to fix something here?" Freddie asked in surprise.

The servant explained that often the poorer workmen cooked their meal of bean porridge over little fires which they built along the street.

"I'm awful sorry I spoiled his supper fire," Freddie said. "I'll help him build another." He hurried off and soon collected a small armful of twigs which he piled neatly in the gutter.

"I wish I could give him something else to eat," the little boy thought. Suddenly he remembered the package of cookies which he had not been able to eat on the plane. Freddie pulled them from his pocket and held them out to the workman. The man's eyes shone as he took the cookies. He smiled and bowed gratefully. Uncle Abdel's servant patted Freddie approvingly on the back and led him into the house.

Inside, the other children were gathered around Mr. Gouda in his study. They all looked worried.

"What's the matter?" asked Freddie, who was eager to tell of his adventure with the fire.

"Salah hasn't come back with the toy horse," Nan explained. "Where have you been so long?"

Freddie hastily told about the workman, his supper, and the water. The others laughed.

"I gave him my cookies," Freddie said promptly.

"That was very nice," Nan remarked.

Mr. Gouda jumped up from his chair. "Why don't you children have some supper yourselves?" He motioned them to the dining room. "I won't be long. I'm going to call Mr. Mal-

"Eeeh! Stop!" the angry man yelled

lakh," he announced. "Perhaps he will know what has happened to Salah."

The children waited anxiously while Uncle Abdel talked to the archaeologist. When he returned from the telephone, he looked disturbed. "I can't understand it," he muttered.

"Has something gone wrong, sir?" Bert inquired.

"Mr. Mallakh says that Salah left his house with the horse two hours ago," Uncle Abdel replied. "He certainly should be here by this time."

"Perhaps someone stopped him," Flossie spoke up. "Did Mr. Mallakh see him go away?"

"That's an idea!" Uncle Abdel remarked. "I'll ask him."

He telephoned the archaeologist again and asked if Salah had actually been seen leaving the house.

"I'll inquire among my servants," Mr. Mallakh offered. Soon he came back with the information. Uncle Abdel listened intently, then exclaimed, "Halif! That's bad!" He thanked his friend and said good-by.

Tom, Terry, and the children eagerly awaited an explanation. Uncle Abdel reported that one of Mr. Mallakh's servants had seen Salah meet a man named Halif and walk off with him.

"Who is Halif?" Nan asked.

"He is a dragoman or guide. Halif has

worked at times for both Mr. Mallakh and me but was discharged for stealing."

"What does this Halif look like?" Bert asked as a thought came to him.

"He is tall and thin and has a white beard."

"Does he wear a black scarab ring?" Nan put in eagerly.

Uncle Abdel smiled. "Yes, Halif considers himself an authority on ancient Egyptian art since he has worked for several archaeologists. He claims his scarab is an old one and very valuable."

"Then Nan and I saw him at the museum this afternoon!" Bert cried out. "And we think he was with Salah!"

Uncle Abdel listened intently while Bert described the incident at the museum. "I can't understand it," he said when the boy had finished. "Salah has been with me for years and has always been reliable. He's not very smart, but I can't believe that he would go off with Halif of his own free will!"

"Perhaps you should notify the police that Salah and the toy horse are missing," Tom suggested.

"I'll call the *politie* at once," the Egyptian said. "The *mamour,* the chief of police, is a friend of mine."

"Maybe we can help you find Salah and the little horse," Flossie piped up when Uncle

Abdel had made his call. "We Bobbseys love to solve mysteries."

"And I've heard they're very good at it, too!" Terry put in.

"You will be doing your Lakeport museum a great service if you can find the antique toy," Mr. Gouda declared.

Danny had been silent, but now he scoffed. "The twins couldn't find anything if it was right in front of them!"

The Bobbseys gave the bully a disgusted glance, then Flossie asked, "What does the little horse look like?"

Uncle Abdel paused. "The horse is about three inches high. It is made of pink clay. There are several thin strips of bright blue, yellow, orange, and red painted across its chest and back. It has wooden wheels which take the place of hoofs. It is a very colorful little antique and it is worth a great deal of money. You see, it is a couple of thousand years old! I hope that Halif has not stolen it."

Bert assured Mr. Gouda that they would try hard to find the clay horse, and Nan added, "First we must find Halif. Have you any idea where we might look for him? Do you know where he lives?"

The Egyptian shook his head. "Halif moves about a great deal. But he used to stay around the

Mena House Hotel on the way to the pyramids at Giza."

"Where is Giza?" Flossie asked. "Can we go there?"

"Giza is not far from Cairo. Many tourists hire camels near the Mena House to ride out to see the pyramids and the Sphinx. I want to take Tom to my office with me tomorrow, but Terry could drive the station wagon if you would like to go look for Halif. It is best to start early in the morning before it gets too hot."

Uncle Abdel told them that the pyramids were royal tombs which had been built thousands of years ago by the rulers of Egypt. "It is said that the largest pyramid at Giza built by King Cheops took one hundred thousand men twenty years to complete.

"As for the Sphinx," Uncle Abdel continued, "it's the largest piece of sculpture ever carved by men's hands!"

"I wish it was morning!" Flossie sighed, when the children had finished their supper. "I want to see all those things!"

Morning finally did arrive and after an early breakfast the children piled into the car with Terry at the wheel. She drove for some distance out along a wide boulevard.

Suddenly Flossie, who was in the front seat, pointed ahead and cried, "Look! Camels!"

In a large field at the side of the road the children saw an amazing sight. There was a long row of kneeling camels and at the head of each one stood a man in a white or blue caftan with white turban.

"Those camels are the ones the tourists ride up to the pyramids," Terry explained. "Perhaps you'll find Halif here."

The children got out of the car and hurried over to the crowd of camels and drivers.

*"Eeh-ah! Eeh-ah!"* Each camel driver called to the youngsters to hire his beast for the trip.

"Isn't this exciting?" Nan turned to Bert.

Freddie and Flossie stayed at Terry's side. The older children walked along the line asking each driver if he knew Halif with the white beard.

"Yes, I know him," one raggedly dressed camel man said. "But I have not seen him lately."

"I don't think we're going to find Halif here," Nan finally said in despair.

They had almost reached the end of the line when Nan motioned her twin to stop. "What is that strange sound?" she asked.

# CHAPTER IV

## A PYRAMID CLUE

THE twins listened intently. The sound came again.

"I think it's a child crying," Nan declared. "But where?"

She peered at the remaining camel drivers. They were laughing and still pointing toward their animals, hoping for passengers.

A short distance beyond Nan saw an Egyptian boy of about ten, dressed in a blue and white pajama-like suit. He was crouched on the ground, his head between his knees, and sobbing bitterly.

"Let's go over and ask him what happened," Nan suggested.

They hurried to the child's side and Nan put a hand on his shoulder. "What's the trouble?" she asked kindly.

The boy raised his head and looked at her with large brown eyes. "Someone steal my Farah!" he sobbed. "I thought she here, but she not!"

"Who is Farah?" asked Bert.

"Farah best racing camel in Cairo!" the boy replied, standing up and drying his tears. "I just make brass tassel for her head."

By this time Terry and the other children had come up. They learned that the boy's name was Ali. His father had a brass shop in Cairo, and the boy went to the mission school near the desert. The camel had been stolen from there.

"My grandfather give me camel when she baby. I train her to race. And Farah take tourists to pyramids. Now she gone!"

"Pretty dumb of you to lose her," Danny muttered.

Flossie spoke up. "We'll find Farah for you, Ali!" she promised.

"Perhaps you can help us, too, Ali," Bert said. "We're looking for a white-bearded dragoman named Halif. Do you know him?"

"Yes," Ali replied. "Halif bad dragoman. He cheat tourists. I see him early this morning riding camel to pyramids."

"You did!" Bert exclaimed.

"I want to ride a camel to the pyramids!" Flossie announced. "Will you take me, Ali?"

The boy looked sad. "Farah gone." Suddenly he brightened. "Maybe my friend let me lead his camel. Then you ride."

"Let's all ride camels," Terry proposed. "You

want to follow Halif to the pyramids and that's
the nicest way to get to them! Going by car is too
modern!"

All the children agreed. Ali found that his
friend was willing to lend him his camel, and
soon each rider was seated on top of one of the
humped beasts. Ali was leading Flossie's camel.
They proudly took their places at the head of the
procession as it moved slowly up the incline. A
few minutes later the pyramids and the huge
crouching figure of the Sphinx came into view.

"I guess," said Flossie to Ali, "the Sph-Sph-
Sphinx is the guard of the pyramids." Ali smiled
and nodded.

When the group reached the base of the largest pyramid, the camel drivers brought their
beasts to a halt. The riders hung onto the saddle
horns as the animals sank clumsily to their knees.

"That was fun!" Flossie declared as she
slipped from the saddle.

"Aren't we going inside the pyramid?" Danny
asked as Ali began to lead the party toward the
Sphinx.

Ali shook his head. "It very dangerous. Not
many tourists try it."

"Have you ever been in?" Bert asked the boy.

"Once, but I not stay long." He shuddered.

"Well, I'm going in," Danny announced. "If
you sissies are scared to go, I'll tell you all about
it when I come out!"

This was too much for Bert and Freddie. "How far in can we go, Ali?" Bert asked.

"To Queen's Chamber," the Egyptian boy replied. "It called that because we think queen buried there. Long time ago thieves enter pyramid. Everything stolen so nobody sure."

"May we go in?" Bert asked Terry eagerly.

The young counselor looked uncertain, then said, "You boys may go only as far as Ali thinks is safe. The rest of us will wait for you here."

Ali led the way through the narrow opening in the Pyramid of Cheops. The corridor inside was about three feet wide and four feet high.

Bert followed Ali. Next came Freddie, with Danny bringing up the rear. The boys crouched and began the descent in single file.

"This air is awful!" Danny complained as they inched along the path. It was hot and musty and the boys breathed with difficulty.

Suddenly there was a whirring sound and a bat brushed past them. "Eeeh!" Danny cried. "I'm getting out of here!" He turned and scrambled back toward the entrance.

"Sissy!" cried Freddie.

The passage was dimly lighted by an occasional electric bulb. Bert noticed several other corridors branching off into inky blackness.

"Now we go up," Ali called back as they came to an incline paved with slippery metal cleats.

A short while later the boys reached a level path. There the roof was slightly higher than in the tunnel they had just come through.

"At end of this Queen's Chamber," Ali told the two Bobbseys.

Suddenly Ali held up one hand, signaling them to halt. "I hear voices!" their young guide whispered. "Wait! I find out who is here."

All the boys listened intently. Two men were talking. They spoke in English with a few words of Arabic. Both were arguing about the price which one of them had agreed to pay for a horse.

"This is a funny place to sell a horse!" Freddie whispered, stifling a laugh.

"I will try to get you more money," one of the men said finally. "Bring the horse to Pompey's Column at *sabaa*. Be careful!"

The men's voices grew nearer as if they were leaving the Queen's Chamber. "We hide," Ali advised. "They sound like bad men!"

Bert felt an opening in the wall behind him and pulled the other two boys into it. They waited breathlessly as the sound of heavy footsteps came closer.

At sight of the first man Bert gasped. By the light of the electric bulb he saw a tall, white-bearded Egyptian. He wore a black scarab ring on his left forefinger. Halif!

Bert peered at the second man. He was not Uncle Abdel's servant Salah.

Bert's thoughts raced. Could the horse Halif had just mentioned be the antique toy? If so, had he stolen it from Salah? And where was Salah now?

"I must find out!" Bert motioned Freddie and Ali to follow him, and crept along the narrow corridor after the men.

When they reached the descending portion, the slippery cleats forced the boys to slow down. At one point Freddie's feet slipped from under him and he fell with a thud. He grunted.

"Ssh!" Bert cautioned.

He was too late. The footsteps ahead of them turned into a run. The boys quickened their pace but reached the entrance just in time to see the two men leap on camels and ride off. Instead of turning toward the city, the men sped away across the sand dunes.

"We've lost them!" Bert said in disgust.

Nan ran up to the boys. "Did you see that man who just came out of the pyramid?" she asked breathlessly. "I'm sure he was Halif!"

Bert nodded gloomily. "I am, too! But he slipped away from us!"

Ali and Bert told Terry and the others what they had overheard in the Queen's Chamber.

"Where is Pompey's Column?" Freddie asked.

"Did you see the man who came out of the pyramid?" Nan
asked breathlessly

"And what is *sabaa?*" Flossie wanted to know.

*"Sabaa,"* said Ali, "is Arabic word for seven."

"And Pompey's Column?" Nan inquired.

Ali looked uncertain. "I think that in Alexandria."

"What does it all mean?" Nan sighed. "Do you believe it's a clue to the missing toy horse?"

"Yes, I do!" Bert stated firmly. "I think that when the other man told Halif to bring the horse to Pompey's Column at *sabaa,* he meant the antique toy horse!"

"Then let's go to Alex," Flossie urged.

"Alexandria, dear," said Nan. She wanted to go there too. "Maybe if we tell Uncle Abdel what you boys overheard, he'll let us go to Alexandria to look for the horse!"

"Come on!" Bert started toward their camels.

Later, when they reached the parking lot and the camel drivers had been paid, the Americans climbed into the car. Nan noticed a wistful expression on Ali's face.

"Would you like to ride with us?" she asked.

Ali beamed and jumped into the front seat next to Freddie. Terry started off.

"It's still early," she said. "Let's stop to see the Mehemet Ali Mosque, a famous Mohammedan church here."

"Ali, do you go to the mosque?" Flossie asked.

Ali smiled. "No." He added, "Mosque built by Egyptian general, Mehemet Ali, hundred year ago. Once a fort here. Mosque built on top."

"Can't I see the fort?" said Freddie, disappointed.

Ali shook his head.

Terry said, "You will find the mosque quite different from our churches."

"How?" Flossie asked.

"You'll see."

The counselor drove up the steep road to the top. After parking the car, she and the children walked across a wide courtyard to the mosque. Near the entrance sat an old Egyptian behind a pile of leather slippers. He motioned Terry and the children to slip the slippers on over their shoes.

"I guess the slippers are worn to protect these beautiful rugs," Terry commented when the group stepped into the mosque. The huge floor was spread with oriental carpets in soft colors.

The children looked around in surprise. There were no seats or other furnishings. Egyptians in native dress knelt around the walls evidently saying their prayers.

A man kneeling a short distance away looked up as the Bobbseys and their friends entered the mosque. Bert stared at him, startled.

"Salah!" he cried.

SALAH! SALAH! SALAH! The name echoed loudly through the huge, quiet building!

# CHAPTER V

## THE TRUNK'S SURPRISE

AS THE name Salah echoed back and forth across the mosque several men arose from their knees and looked around uncertainly.

Flossie whispered, "Are they all named Salah?"

"You sure made yourself heard, Bert!" Danny remarked.

Bert reddened. "I didn't mean to make so much noise," he confessed, "and that man isn't Salah after all!"

"This place very famous for echo," Ali told Bert. "Even well in courtyard has one."

Terry motioned that they should leave and ushered the children back to the car. The counselor said, "Ali, are you going home or to the mission? We'll take you there."

"I go to mission for short time."

He directed her to the school, and the twins

thought it a very nice place. The white concrete building stood inside a colorful garden of flowers and palm trees. They met the principal, Mr. Lanier, a Frenchman.

After introductions were over, he invited the visitors to luncheon. "Would you like a meal desert style?" he asked, his eyes twinkling.

"Oh, yes," the twins answered, but Danny scowled and said nothing.

Mr. Lanier led the guests into the plain, white-walled dining room with several long, large tables. There were no plates on it, just large spoons.

The mission cook brought in round flat pieces of bread and a huge bowl of stew. The delicious aroma floated throughout the room. He spread out a thick white paper cloth.

"It's a little messy, but a lot of fun!" Mr. Lanier assured Terry, who seemed curious.

A round flat piece of bread was placed before each visitor.

"Now we spoon some of the stew onto our bread," the principal explained. "We eat as much of it as we want to and when we are through, we eat our bread."

"You mean we eat our plate?" Freddie asked and he nodded. The children gaily ate their stew and the "plates."

"This is super!" Bert said as he munched on a huge chunk of bread.

"For dessert, well—" Mr. Lanier paused as the matronly cook brought in two large plates of cookies, oranges, dates, and bananas.

"These are called pistachio cookies," Mr. Lanier said. "And now the biggest surprise!"

He opened one of the closets in the room and carefully placed a strange object in the center of the table. "This, my friends, is a large spoon."

"But that looks like the statue of a duck being held up by a girl," Bert said.

"If you notice, the duck is wooden and carved out in the center!" the principal said.

The little maid swimming behind it had jewels on her forehead and neck. Her two thin wooden arms were stretched out in front of her, holding onto the gay turquoise-and-brown duck.

"The piece is very, very old," Mr. Lanier said.

The cook filled the duck with a thick white liquid.

"Camel's milk for everyone!" the principal announced.

Bert and Nan screwed up their faces. "What do you think it tastes like?" Nan whispered to her brother.

Bert shrugged.

"The Arab children," Mr. Lanier went on, "are brought up on this milk. It is very rich, richer than the cows' milk you probably are used to."

Danny scowled. "Aw, it tastes like chicken jelly!"

"Shush!" Flossie scolded him.

Mr. Lanier passed around the fruit, and the children particularly liked the rich brown dates.

"You know the Arab tribes use every part of the date tree," the mission teacher went on. "They don't just eat the dates. Their tent poles are made from the trunk of the tree. The wide palm leaves are woven into mats for the floor of the tents."

The visitors thanked Mr. Lanier for the luncheon, then Bert asked, "Could Ali go to Mr. Gouda's house with us? We want to visit Alexandria, and maybe take Ali with us."

"That would be a nice trip," said Mr. Lanier, "but perhaps he should stay here and hunt for Farah. Ali, I think you'd better call your father and ask him."

After a few minutes, the little boy returned, grinning. "I go Uncle Abdel's house with you."

When they arrived, a servant told them that their host was waiting for them in the parlor.

Eager to tell Uncle Abdel about their morning's adventure, the children hurried into the room. In the center glistened a sunken marble pool.

The parlor was furnished in traditional Egyptian style with straight, heavy chairs and tables intricately carved and inlaid with mother-of-pearl. The wall at one end was completely covered by a wooden cabinet which reached to the ceiling.

Uncle Abdel and Tom stood in front of the cabinet. "Come in, children," Mr. Gouda called. "I was showing Tom my collection of pottery."

The shelves were filled with Chinese bowls, Japanese dishes, and Turkish glass.

"They're bee-yoo-ti-full!" Flossie exclaimed, running up to look.

"Some are very valuable," their host said. "I have been collecting them for years!"

"Aren't we going to ask about going to Alexandria?" Freddie spoke up impatiently.

"Going to Alexandria?" Uncle Abdel asked.

"Yes, sir," Bert spoke up. "You see it was like this—" He introduced Ali and told about the conversation they had overheard in the pyramid. "One of the men was Halif!"

"We thought," Nan added, "that if we went to Alexandria, we might find Halif. Maybe he'll try to sell your antique horse to someone there!"

Mr. Gouda thought a moment. "I wish you could find it, but I am afraid there is only a very slim chance. You would enjoy a visit to Alexandria, however. I am sorry but I can spare only one car to take you."

At once Tom said, "The Bobbseys are the detectives. Let them go. Danny and I will do some sightseeing here, and Terry can drive the twins to Alexandria."

"Oh, all right," Danny replied grudgingly. "I'm sick of watching them play detectives, anyway."

Ali could not be included because he had not received his father's permission.

"Pack your things to stay overnight and be ready to leave in an hour," Mr. Gouda said.

The Bobbseys collected their belongings, then said good-by to Ali. "We'll look for your camel when we come back from Alexandria," Flossie promised. Ali looked forlorn but started off down the street whistling.

It was almost three when Terry and the twins climbed into the car. "You'll have to hurry if you want to get to Alexandria by seven o'clock," Uncle Abdel cautioned her. "It's a long drive."

The small twins sat in front while Bert and Nan climbed into the back with two of the suitcases. The rest had been stowed in the trunk.

Soon after leaving the city they reached the desert. There was nothing in sight for miles but yellow sand and a mud shack here and there. In the distance occasional camels and their riders were silhouetted against the sky.

"Whew! I'm hot!" Bert exclaimed, mopping his face. "It must be at least a hundred degrees!"

Nan did not answer. "Listen! I thought I heard someone call our names," she said.

"There's no one around but us," Bert answered.

*Thump, Thump!* A knocking sound came from the rear of the car. Terry pulled to the side of the road.

"Do you think we have a flat tire?" she asked anxiously.

"We'll look!" Bert and Nan got out of the car and walked around to the back. The tires were all right.

"Bert! Nan!" came a muffled voice.

"That sound is coming from the trunk of the car!" Nan declared. "May we have the key, Terry?"

Bert unlocked the trunk and opened it.

"Ali!" Nan cried.

The Egyptian boy tumbled out, half unconscious from the heat. When Terry heard Nan's exclamation, she and the younger twins jumped out of the car and joined the others.

"Oh, Ali, you poor child!" the counselor exclaimed.

The fresh air revived him quickly, and Nan gave him a cool drink from the Thermos jug.

"Ali!" Nan cried

"How'd you get in the trunk?" Freddie asked.

"After Bert put bags in, he not close top right away. I climb inside." Ali grinned.

Terry looked annoyed. "Whatever gave you the idea of hiding in the trunk?"

"No time to ask father. I know you not let me go without he say okay."

"Oh, Ali, you never should have come away without your father's permission," the counselor said.

Ali looked pleadingly at Terry and the Bobbseys. "Please, I go to Alexandria with you! No make me go back! I help you find Pompey's Column!"

Terry patted him on the shoulder. "You may come along. But at the first opportunity we must find a telephone for you to call your father at his shop."

Ali's brown face beamed with happiness. He climbed into the back seat between Bert and Nan.

"What time is it, Terry?" Nan asked.

Terry glanced at her watch. "It's six o'clock. I think we'll have time to go to the hotel before finding Pompey's Column. We should get word to Ali's father that he is with us."

At the hotel which Uncle Abdel had recommended, Terry engaged two rooms—one for her and the girls, the other for the boys. Next she telephoned Mr. Gouda, and Ali talked to him. Uncle Abdel promised to send word to Ali's father to tell him where the boy was.

Flossie had been jumping up and down impatiently.

"Come on!" she urged. "We'll be late!"

"Do you know where Pompey's Column is, Ali?" Terry asked.

The Egyptian boy shook his head. "But I find out," he promised.

When the group reached the lobby again, Ali talked to the doorman in Arabic.

"Man give me map of city," Ali told Terry. "Column marked on it."

A fifteen-minute drive took the group outside the modern city.

"There it is!" Freddie pointed to a tall column which stood on a small rise of land. It was made of polished red granite and glowed in the late afternoon light. A fence surrounded the area, which was strewn with fragments of broken columns.

Bert tried the gate. "It's locked!" Then he read the sign near the gate: *Open daily from 9 A.M. to 5 P.M.*

"What shall we do?" Nan asked anxiously. "It's almost seven o'clock."

"Halif probably arranged to meet that other man here," Bert surmised, "because he knew the monument would be closed and no one would be around. Let's hide down there." He pointed toward a hollow on the far side of the column.

Quickly they made their way to the place and crouched at the foot of the low hill where the column stood. They waited silently for what seemed a long time.

Finally Nan whispered to Terry, "What time is it?"

Terry looked at her watch. "Seven-thirty. I guess no one is coming."

Bert and Nan stood up and stretched, while Freddie and Flossie began to chase each other over the rocky ground.

"Maybe Halif meant seven o'clock in the morning," Bert suggested.

Freddie overheard his brother. "Let's come back then," he said. "I'm so hungry now!"

In the car again, Terry drove the disappointed children back to the hotel and a late dinner. The next morning after a good breakfast they all returned to the Column. Once more Terry and the children took their places in the hollow.

When no one had appeared by eight o'clock, the counselor spoke up. "I'm afraid you children are on the wrong trail. We'd better see a little of Alexandria and then return to Cairo."

"Oh, Terry!" Flossie wailed. "We want to catch the man who took Uncle Abdel's horse!"

"Can't we stay until tomorrow?" Freddie pleaded.

"Halif might have meant seven o'clock to-night," Ali pointed out.

Terry relented. "All right. We'll try again tonight. But if he doesn't come this time, I think you should give up."

When they reached the car, a peddler with a cart full of souvenirs was waiting for them. He approached the group eagerly.

"You like souvenir of Egypt?" the man said. He picked up the tiny brass head of a woman wearing a high crown. "This is Nefertiti, ancient queen of Egypt," he declared. "You like?"

Nan had been turning over some pieces of jewelry on the cart. Suddenly she saw a black scarab ring. Could it possibly have any connection with Halif?

Picking up the ring, Nan asked, "Can you—?"

Before she could say another word, the peddler had grabbed the ring from her hand, picked up the handles of the cart, and scurried away!

# CHAPTER VI

## SMALL CLEOPATRA

"CATCH him!" Flossie cried, jumping up and down in excitement.

With Freddie at his heels, Ali raced after the peddler. They soon caught up with him. He and Ali held a spirited conversation. Then the man trundled his cart away. Ali and Freddie came back to Bert and the girls.

"What did he say?" Nan asked breathlessly.

Ali grinned. "Man saving scarab ring for wife," he said. "When you pick it up, he afraid you want to buy. He not know English, so he run away!"

Nan sighed. "I thought perhaps it was a clue to Halif!"

"Maybe Halif will come to the Column tonight!" Freddie consoled her. "What are we going to do now?"

"I'd like to buy an Egyptian costume to take

home," Nan remarked. "Could we go to some shops, Terry?"

"I want a costume too!" Flossie piped up.

"All right," said Terry. "We came through a section of the city where there were some nice-looking stores. Suppose we go back there."

A short time later she parked the car near a busy intersection.

"What is that man doing?" Freddie asked, looking ahead.

"He getting haircut and shave," Ali explained.

An old jalopy was parked along the curb. An Egyptian wearing a dirty yellow caftan was seated on the running board of the car. Another man, who was dressed in a dark gray and black caftan, was cutting the seated man's hair with a dull pair of scissors.

"That's a barbershop?" Bert exclaimed.

"Yes," Ali said.

"How come there's no big red and white striped pole?" Nan asked laughingly.

"That's a traveling barbershop, I guess, Nan!" Terry said, laughing. "Let's go!"

She led the way up the street with Nan and Flossie. Ali trailed them. Bert and Freddie brought up the rear.

When they reached the traffic light, it was green. Terry and the girls hurried across the street. Ali fell into step with Bert. Thinking Freddie was beside them, the boys also made the crossing.

But Freddie had seen something else which interested him. On a grassy little island at the meeting of five streets the traffic officer sat in a high, elevated glass-walled booth. An iron ladder was hooked to it.

Freddie stood on the curb and gazed at the strange little building. "If I could sit up in a place like that," he thought, "I'd be a traffic policeman instead of a fireman!"

The stream of cars and trucks slackened for a minute. The officer peered down at the little boy who looked up at him so admiringly.

The officer smiled and beckoned to Freddie to join him. Delighted, the little boy scrambled up the iron steps into the glass booth.

"You are an American?" the officer asked.

Freddie nodded eagerly, his eyes fixed on the little stand in front of the policeman. "Do you punch those buttons to change the lights?" he asked.

"Yes. Sometimes there is more traffic than at other times, so I can keep the cars moving by these signals."

Freddie looked enviously at the panel of buttons. "Could I punch just one?" he pleaded.

The officer looked at the streets coming into

the intersection. The traffic flow was light. "Push this one." He pointed.

The little boy grinned as the traffic came to a halt along one of the streets and started up on another.

"This is great!" he thought and quickly pushed another button.

With a screech of brakes, cars and trucks came to a sudden stop.

*Beep! Beep!*

People looked to see what the trouble was.

Freddie was frightened. "Wh—what did I do?" he asked in a shaky voice.

"You made the light change too quickly," the annoyed officer replied. "However, no harm has been done, but I think you have directed enough traffic for today."

"I—I guess so," Freddie agreed. "Thank you for showing me." He scurried down the steps.

Back at the curb, Freddie looked up at the glass booth. With a friendly wave of his hand, the officer turned the light green for the little boy to cross the street.

Terry and the other children were waiting frantically on the other side. "Where did you go?" Bert asked. "You suddenly disappeared."

"I was directing traffic," Freddie replied, puffing out his chest and grinning.

"You what?" Terry gasped.

Freddie told them of his adventure and pointed toward his friend the officer, who waved to the group.

"I think you were mean not to take me," Flossie pouted. "I want to be a traffic policeman too!"

"I think one Bobbsey was enough!" Terry said. "Now how about finding those costumes you wanted?"

The counselor and the children walked along the busy street, peering into the shopwindows. Finally Nan stopped in front of one.

"This is a rug store," she said, "but I think I see some clothes in the rear."

A stout man greeted them as they entered the long, narrow shop. "May I show you some carpets?"

"They're lovely!" Nan said as she looked at the rolls of richly colored carpet.

"Our Egyptian carpets are famous," the man said. "We sell the finest rugs in Alexandria."

Noticing that Nan and Flossie were interested, he continued, "Have you heard what Cleopatra did when the Roman general Julius Caesar refused to see her?"

"No!"

"Well, she ordered herself to be rolled up in a length of carpet which was to be presented to him. When the carpet was unrolled before Caesar, the queen tumbled out!"

"How 'citing!" Flossie's blue eyes sparkled.

"We are looking for Egyptian costumes to take home. Have you any?"

"Certainly! Just step to the rear of the store and I will show you some *galabias*."

The friendly proprietor pulled out several straight, ankle-length gowns worn by Egyptian men and then the wide-sleeved robes called galabias.

"These go over the caftans," he explained. "But most boys and young men wear these suits."

He held up a two-piece garment of blue and white striped cotton. "Like this young man's." He smiled at Ali.

Bert and Freddie decided the suits looked too much like their own pajamas. Each selected a galabia and a white turban.

The shop owner told the Americans that city women in Egypt wore clothes similar to the western women. "Those in the country wear only black dresses and cover their heads with black shawls."

"What do you think, Floss?" Nan asked, turning to consult her little sister. Flossie was not there.

At that moment a customer came into the shop. "I have had a special carpet woven for this gentleman," the owner explained to his visitors. "Would you like to see it?"

Terry and the children followed the proprietor to the front of the shop where he greeted his distinguished-looking customer. "I have your carpet ready," the shop owner said proudly. "I will show you."

He took hold of the end of a roll which lay against the wall and with a flourish sent the length unrolling across the floor. A second later the onlookers gasped.

*Flossie Bobbsey tumbled out at the end of the roll!*

"Flossie!" Nan cried. "How did you get in there?"

The little girl struggled to her feet. "Freddie helped me. I was playing Cleopatra!" She coughed. "And I thought no one was ever coming to unroll me!"

Everybody laughed over the incident. The customer took his carpet and left, still chuckling over "Cleopatra."

Nan and Flossie returned to the back of the shop. "We look like two black crows," Nan decided as they wound black shawls around their heads and shoulders. "Won't Mother be surprised when she sees us in these!"

Terry now took the children to lunch in a nearby hotel. When they had finished eating, the counselor suggested, "How about a swim?"

"Oh, yes!" the children chorused.

Terry drove out of the city along the shore of

"Flossie!" Nan cried. "How did you get in there?"

the Mediterranean until they came to a modern-looking beach club. They rented bathing suits and before long were frolicking in the cool blue water.

Warm breezes floated around the children and over the sun-bleached sand. "Isn't this dreamy?" Nan said as she spied the glistening white buildings.

"We'd better get dressed if we're to be at Pompey's Column by seven," Bert said a little later.

It was shortly before seven when the young detectives reached the Column. Quickly they took their places in the little hollow.

"I hope Halif comes tonight!" Flossie said.

"Ssh! Quiet!" Bert cautioned.

Just then a taxi drove up and a short, heavy-set man got out. He ordered the driver to wait, then strolled toward the fence. A second later a tall, white-bearded man in a brown caftan and turban walked toward him. He carried a stuffed toy camel under his arm.

"Halif!" Bert hissed.

Flossie giggled. "Why does he have a toy camel? Does he play with it?"

Nan held her finger to her lips. "Ssh!"

The two men greeted each other. Halif seemed to be asking the gruff-looking man a question. At the reply he burst into a storm of Arabic.

"But where is Uncle Abdel's antique horse?" Nan asked. "Do you suppose Halif didn't steal it after all?"

"That other man seems to want to take the toy camel," Bert observed. "I'll bet the horse is hidden inside it!"

Finally Halif appeared to give in. He handed the toy camel to the other man. As he put out his hand to take it, Ali stood up and shouted:

"That man steal Farah! He wear brass tassel on wrist I make for my camel!"

# CHAPTER VII

## CAMEL FISHING

AT Ali's cry the two men looked in fright toward the hollow where the children crouched in hiding.

"Come on." The short man grabbed the toy camel and dashed to the waiting taxi. Halif followed, his gown flapping around his ankles.

Bert, Freddie, and Ali took up the chase, but before they could reach the fleeing men the Egyptians leaped into the taxi and sped off.

"Hurry!" Terry called. "Maybe we can catch them!"

The children jumped into their own car, and Terry roared off after the speeding cab. She followed it around corner after corner. Occasionally she would lose it, but caught up again when heavy traffic forced the taxi to slow down.

"You're a great driver, Terry!" Bert said admiringly.

The young counselor smiled. "I'm not going to lose that antique horse if I can help it!"

"Do you really think the horse is in the toy camel?" Flossie asked her big brother.

"Yes, I do," Bert insisted. "He put the horse inside the camel so no one would know what he was carrying."

"We must catch him!" Nan declared.

"I imagine we're getting near the docks," Terry observed. "I see some ships' stacks ahead."

Their next turn brought them into a street filled with trucks which were piled high with bales and crates and moved along slowly.

"There's our taxi!" Freddie cried. He pointed ahead. The taxi had slowed almost to a stop. The man carrying the stuffed camel jumped out, and the cab drove off with Halif.

Bert and Ali leaped from the car and raced to the dockside. They were just in time to see the man with the camel jump onto the deck of a ship and disappear inside.

As Bert started to follow, Ali caught his arm. "Better to get *politie*," he said. "He find man."

"I guess you're right," Bert agreed, "and there's a policeman over in that shed." He walked up to the officer and explained what had happened.

The policeman looked uncertain but said he would find out what was going on. He went aboard with Bert and Ali and spoke to the captain and other officers. Ali interpreted for the twins. "Nobody here with toy camel," he said.

"Where did he go?" Bert asked.

"The man must have left the ship when you were talking to me," the policeman answered. "That ship sails for Beirut in an hour."

As the two boys walked back to the car, Ali asked, "What you do now, Bert?"

"I'm not giving up!" Bert replied. "I'm sure that man is still on the ship!"

Terry and the others were waiting impatiently to hear what had happened. Bert told the story. "I want to go on that boat. Will you take us, Terry, if Uncle Abdel gives us permission?"

The counselor agreed. "We'll have to hurry," she said, "if the ship leaves in an hour."

They drove back to the hotel and Bert telephoned Uncle Abdel while the others waited breathlessly. In a few minutes Bert came from the booth, a broad smile on his face.

"Uncle Abdel is really great!" he declared. "He says we can go ahead to Beirut in Lebanon, and then fly back to Cairo. His chauffeur will come here to pick up our car."

"Hooray!" Freddie shouted. "Let's go!"

Terry told the children to pack while she made arrangements for the overnight passage to Beirut.

When they reached the ship, they were

greeted by the captain. "Glad to have you aboard!" he boomed. "Mr. Abdel Gouda telephoned. He is a good friend of mine and told me to take good care of you!"

A steward offered to show the twins and their friends to the cabins where they would sleep. The others went off, but the twins held back. They had heard some shouts from the water and walked to the rail to see who was shouting. There was a man in a large rowboat at the side of the ship. It was filled with Egyptian souvenirs—camel saddles, bright scarves, leather hassocks, and brass articles. At the very end of the boat was a pile of stuffed toy camels.

"Maybe that's where our camel went!" Freddie said excitedly.

The peddler in the boat noticed the children's interest. "You want stuffed camel?" he called. "Very nice. Very cheap."

The twins peered at the array of toy camels. One at the edge of the heap was gray with red tassels.

"That looks like the one Halif had!" Nan said. She pointed it out to the peddler.

The man quickly picked up a tan stuffed animal and put it in a basket attached to a rope flung over the railing. He began to hoist it up pulley style. Bert shook his head and pointed to the gray camel. But the peddler continued to pull up the basket.

"We'll look at this to please him," said Nan.

"And then send it back," Freddie spoke up.

When the toy arrived, he said, "This is the wrong one all right." The others agreed.

"I'm sure it's that gray one," said Nan, and pointed to the camel in the rowboat.

Freddie replaced the tan camel in the basket and dropped it to the rowboat. The peddler spread his arms in a gesture of despair.

Nan leaned over the rail and pointed to the gray camel. "That one!" she called.

Once more the man pulled up the basket. This time the gray camel was in it.

Freddie grabbed the toy eagerly while Nan put some money in the basket and sent it down again. The twins were excited as they felt the toy. "There's something in here!" Freddie shouted.

"Hurry up and open it!" Flossie begged.

Bert was not convinced the toy horse was inside but took out his penknife. "We'll soon see," he said.

He slit the stuffed camel and felt inside. There was nothing in it but the stuffing!

"Never mind," Nan said consolingly. "It was a good idea."

There were several deep whistles from the ship. The peddler rowed off, and the vessel began to move slowly out of the harbor.

Shortly afterward the announcement that dinner was being served came over the loud-

"You want stuffed camel?" the peddler asked

speaker. When the meal was finished, the children met in the lounge.

Freddie and Flossie were so sleepy that they had difficulty keeping their eyes open. Terry smiled. "To bed, to bed, sleepyheads," she teased. "We dock in Lebanon early tomorrow and you'll want to be fresh for your detective work!"

The younger twins agreed reluctantly and were soon asleep in their cabins.

"Let's separate and search the ship thoroughly for that man," Bert proposed to Ali and Nan.

They decided that Ali, in his Egyptian clothes, would be less noticeable than Bert or Nan, so he would search the kitchen and engine room. He scurried along the main deck to the stairway and went down. Meanwhile, Bert took the upper and boat decks, while Nan looked through the public rooms for the mysterious Egyptian.

Half an hour later the three came into the lounge where Terry was reading. "Any luck?" she asked.

The searchers shook their heads. They had checked every possible hiding place. None of them had seen the strange man.

"I hope we didn't make a mistake taking this ship," Nan remarked. "Perhaps the man did get off in Alexandria!"

Terry said, "If he is on the ship, he must be in

a cabin. We may spot him tomorrow when he gets off."

They all went to bed and fell asleep.

At once Bert dreamed of chasing a man. Bert was just about to catch him when the man turned into a camel and sped off across the desert! The boy awoke with a start.

A shadowy figure was just leaving his cabin!

# CHAPTER VIII

### A SERIOUS CHARGE

"WAIT!" Bert cried, but the door slammed behind the figure before he could leap from bed.

Freddie and Ali, who occupied the other two bunks in the cabin, woke up. "What's the matter?" Freddie asked. He sat up and rubbed his eyes.

"Someone was in this cabin and I'm going to find him!" Bert hurriedly put on his robe and slippers and went out.

Freddie began to climb down from his upper bunk. "I'm going too! Come on!"

"We stay here," said Ali. "Maybe man come back. Steal."

Freddie lay down again. "All right. We'll pretend to be asleep and if he comes in, we'll capture him!" The little boy pulled the blanket up under his chin and closed his eyes.

A few minutes later the door of the darkened

cabin opened slowly. A figure walked quietly into the room. Freddie waited breathlessly.

When the strange figure came to a halt beside his bunk, the little boy suddenly rolled out on top of the dark form, pulling it to the floor!

"What—?" Bert struggled to his feet and snapped on the light. "Freddie! What's the big idea?"

Freddie grinned. "We thought you were a burglar! Did you find the man?"

"No. I looked along the corridors but couldn't see him. I wonder what he wanted in here." Bert made a quick examination of his suitcase, but nothing was missing.

Since there seemed to be no answer to Bert's question, the three boys went back to sleep. The next morning the ship bustled with activity. All luggage was put in the corridors to be collected by the steward. Breakfast was served early.

While finishing their warm muffins and jam, Terry and the children heard a commotion on the foredeck.

"What is noise?" Ali asked as he scurried to the railing.

Freddie pointed. "That boy's paddling in a garbage can!"

"Looks like an old gasoline tank to me," Nan said, grinning.

"He's keeping us from landing," Terry put in.

Suddenly an officer shouted some words in Arabic and motioned the boy away from the ship.

With two pieces of metal tied to his hands like paddles, the little boy made his way to the dock where he was helped ashore.

The ship finally docked, but no one was allowed to get off until given a landing pass by the Lebanese authorities.

Freddie, Flossie, and Ali leaned over the rail and watched the doings on the dock. There was a line of automobiles with "For Hire" signs on them. The drivers were huddled into little groups talking and waiting for the ship's passengers to disembark.

"Why can't we get off?" Flossie asked impatiently.

Suddenly Freddie grabbed Nan's arm. "Look!" he cried. "That man just jumped ashore from that lower door in the ship—and he has a brass tassel on his wrist!"

"And he acts as if he has something up his sleeve," Flossie exclaimed. "The toy camel!"

Flossie and Freddie watched the heavy-set man. He was wearing a white robe and a white veil covering the back of his head and shoulders. When he approached the line of waiting cars, Freddie ran to the top of the gangplank.

"I'm going to stop him!" he called back to Nan.

The Lebanese officer on guard caught Freddie by the shoulder. "Just a minute! Where is your landing card?"

"My brother's inside getting it," Freddie replied, "but I want to catch that man!"

"Stand back," the officer said firmly. "You cannot land without a card."

In the meantime Bert, Nan, and Terry had collected the landing cards for the party. They were just about to step out onto the deck when an announcement came over the loudspeaker.

"Will Bert Bobbsey please come to the purser's office?"

"Oh, Bert," Nan said worriedly, "why do they want you?"

Bert shrugged.

When he entered the purser's office, he saw his overnight bag on the officer's desk. "Is something wrong?" Bert asked.

"I am not sure." The purser explained that one of the stewards had noticed a note written in Arabic pasted to the side of the boy's bag. "It makes a very serious accusation against you," the officer said.

"Against me?" Bert asked in surprise. "What have I done?"

"The note warns us that you are carrying a valuable piece stolen from an excavation. We must examine your bag. If we find the article, I have no choice but to place you under arrest."

"You're certainly welcome to look in my bag," Bert declared. "I don't know anything about any stolen articles." He handed the key to the purser.

The officer opened the bag and carefully examined everything inside, then closed it.

"I am very sorry about this, Bert," he said. "But you understand I couldn't take a chance that you might be carrying stolen property. Now you and your party may go ashore. I hope you will enjoy your visit to Lebanon."

Bert hurried out to the others.

Nan was indignant when she heard her twin's story. "But who would accuse you of such a thing?"

"That man who came into our cabin last night!" Bert answered.

"It could have been the camel man," Nan suggested. "He probably wanted to keep us from following him."

"We saw him!" Flossie spoke up. "He went over to talk to those drivers. He had a white veil over his head!"

"That is a typical Syrian head covering," Terry told her. "It is called *kuffiyah* and is worn to protect the head and neck from the hot sun."

"We've probably lost him," Bert admitted, "but let's see what we can find out on the dock."

Terry and the children hurried ashore. They

"Just a minute! Where is your landing card?" the officer asked

walked over to the drivers who had not yet succeeded in getting passengers. Ali questioned the men about the stranger with the brass tassel on his wrist.

Finally one of the drivers spoke up. Ali listened intently as the man spoke in Arabic. Then the Egyptian boy turned to the Bobbseys.

"This man remember one who wear my tassel," he explained. "He say man in great hurry. He rent car to drive himself."

"Does he know where the man was going?" Nan asked.

"Damascus."

"How far is that?" Bert inquired.

Ali questioned the driver again. The man explained that Damascus was in Syria and it was about a three-hour drive through the mountains.

"Let's follow him!" Bert looked questioningly at Terry.

The young counselor grinned. "I'm game!" she said. "We've come too far to give up now! But see if you can get a car with a driver who speaks English, Ali."

The Egyptian boy hurried off and the twins could see him bargaining with the men. Presently he returned with one who was middle-aged.

"This is Kassan," the boy announced. "He drive us to Damascus. He not charge much."

As the group followed Kassan toward his car,

Bert had an idea. He asked Ali, "Can you find out what kind of car the camel man hired, Ali?"

Ali ran back to the group of drivers. When he came back, he said the man had taken an American make car—a four-door sedan painted gray.

"Do you think you can catch him, Kassan?" Freddie asked as he and Ali climbed into the front seat.

The black-haired man gave him a big smile. "I try!" he promised. "We must cross border into Syria. Perhaps man be delayed there and we catch him!"

As the car began to move toward the dock entrance, Flossie noticed a fruit vendor. His cart was piled high with tiny green bananas.

"Oh, look!" she cried. "What funny bananas!"

"Those are very good to have on trip," Kassan said. "I get you some." He stopped the car and called to the peddler. A moment later Kassan passed a bunch of bananas back to Terry.

"I want one now!" Freddie insisted. Terry broke off a banana for each of the children and one for Kassan. "We'll keep the rest for later," she said.

"Yumm! They are good!" Flossie said, popping a piece of the fruit into her mouth.

Kassan drove through the city and out to the

country. In a few minutes the road began to wind into the mountains. Soon all that could be seen were flocks of sheep and here and there a shepherd's hut huddled against the rocky side of a mountain.

After a two-hour drive through this desolate country, Kassan pointed ahead. A wide gateway stretched across the road with a booth at each side. On the arch above the road was a sign in English, French, and Arabic:

WELCOME TO SYRIA.

There were two lines of cars waiting to pass the border.

"How long will this take?" Bert asked Kassan.

He shrugged. "Sometime we go through fast, sometime slow. Who knows?"

Bert got out and walked up the line of cars. He was back in a minute. "There's a gray American car in the other line almost at the barrier! A man in a kuffiyah is driving," he told Kassan.

As he spoke, the line began to move and Bert climbed inside again. The children fidgeted as Kassan inched slowly forward.

"We're almost up to the camel man's car!" Flossie observed a few minutes later.

Nan gasped when the two cars arrived at the check points together. They would surely catch the man now!

The official came slowly from the booth and

began to check Kassan's papers. Then he signaled for him to get out and open the trunk of the car.

Bert groaned. "We'll never get that man with the toy camel if we have to stop here so long!"

After a thorough search of the car and a long inspection of the papers, the official finally motioned Kassan to go ahead. The children breathed sighs of relief. But as Kassan started the car, the official asked him another question.

While he answered, the gray American car passed the barrier and sped down the road!

# CHAPTER IX

## MOUNTAIN CHASE

"HURRY! Catch him!" the twins begged.

But the official continued to ask questions and the gray car disappeared in the distance. Finally the man waved Kassan on. He put on speed and the sedan roared ahead.

"I am sorry," Kassan said, "but I could not hurry soldier."

Once more the road wound through mountains. As the Bobbsey car reached the top of an incline, Bert pointed out an automobile speeding along far ahead.

"I think that is the man," he declared.

Kassan drove as fast as he dared over the curving road. Several times the twins caught sight of the other car. The distance between them appeared to be growing shorter.

"He's turning off!" Nan called out presently.

Their driver speeded up. "If he turned on side

road, we catch him. Nobody can go fast on bad road."

A few minutes later he reached the narrow side road. He turned and the car lurched up the rocky path.

Terry and the children bounced around helplessly as Kassan twisted along the mountain trail. It grew narrower and narrower and steeper and steeper. Finally it ended abruptly in a rocky pasture!

Terry said, "The camel man certainly didn't come this far!" She got out of the car to stretch and walk around. "And there was no house along the way where he could have stopped!"

Bert climbed from the back seat and stared at the ground. "No car came here before us," he decided. "There aren't any tire marks."

He went to the edge of the field and looked down into the valley. "There's a car down on the main road!" he exclaimed. "And I'm sure it's the same one we've been chasing!"

"But how could it be?" Nan protested. "We saw it turn off!"

"He must have driven onto the side road and hidden the car behind some rocks," Terry suggested. "Then after we passed him he went back to the highway. He certainly fooled us!"

Bert climbed back into the car. "Come on!" he called. "Maybe we can still catch him!"

Kassan managed to turn the car around and

drove back down the rocky trail. Everyone gave a sigh of relief when they reached the smooth highway. There were no other vehicles in sight.

"I'm hungry!" Freddie cried.

"There is small village ahead," Kassan said. "Maybe we find something to eat there."

"We might as well stop," Bert agreed. "I'm sure that other car is in Damascus by now!"

A turn in the road a little farther on brought them to a village. The main street was deserted except for a few men playing cards under a tree. Kassan pulled up before a small building with a restaurant sign.

"Look!" Ali cried. "The gray car!"

The sedan was parked beside a forlorn-looking donkey tied to a pole in front of the restaurant.

"Now we've caught him!" Bert cried. He threw open the door and the children dashed in. A second later they stopped in dismay. The room was filled with men, all in long white gowns and kuffiyahs.

"Which one is *our* man?" Flossie whispered to her sister.

Nan looked uncertain. "I—I don't know. With those Syrian headdresses on, I can't see their faces!"

"Let's walk around and try to find the man with the tassel on his wrist," Bert suggested.

The children made a slow circuit of the room, peering at each native to see if one wore a brass tassel. As Nan went past one table a man got up hurriedly and walked toward the door.

Nan grabbed Bert and pointed the man out. "I think he's carrying something in his sleeve," she declared.

As the twins watched, the man stopped to pay his bill and then left.

"Maybe I can find out who he is," said Bert. He went up to the restaurant owner and asked about the person who had just left.

"His name is Omir and he works for a man in the Damascus bazaar named Attiyah," the owner answered. Bert reported this to the others.

Just then Ali ran up. "Man went in gray car!" he cried.

"Our camel man is named Omir!" Bert exclaimed.

The twins waved frantically to Terry, who was at the far end of the room. She hurried forward and they all ran from the restaurant. They reached the street just in time to glimpse the gray car speeding down the highway.

"Now we can follow him and see where he goes in Damascus!" Nan said excitedly as they all scrambled into their automobile.

"I'm still hungry!" Freddie wailed. "We never did get anything to eat!"

"I'm hungry too!" Flossie echoed her twin.

Terry took the bananas from the ledge behind the back seat. "Eat the rest of these," she urged. "They'll keep you from starving!"

The American car had a more powerful motor than the one Kassan was driving, and it was all he could do to keep Omir in sight.

Bert and Nan were in the front seat now. They looked intently ahead while Kassan concentrated on the driving. The road was still winding and mountainous.

In the back seat Ali began to tell the younger twins how to say a few things in Arabic. They giggled as they repeated the strange-sounding words.

"*Keef halak?* That means, 'How are you?'" Ali said.

"*Keef halak,*" the twins repeated.

"I am *mabsoot,*" Ali replied.

"What does that mean?" Freddie asked.

"*Mabsoot* means 'happy.'"

"*Keef halak,* Flossie?" Terry asked teasingly.

Flossie giggled. "*Mabsoot,* thank you."

"You mean, *mabsoot, shockran,*" Ali corrected her. "*Shockran* is 'thank you.'"

When Freddie and Flossie had asked everyone how they were, Ali said, "Now you say *khatrak.* That is good-by!"

"*Khatrak!*" everyone chorused.

"He's carrying something in his sleeve!" Nan declared

"This is sure a hairpin curve," Bert observed a moment later, as the car swung around a sharp turn. Then he gasped.

Running down from the hill and out onto the road just ahead of the car was a large flock of sheep! Some of the animals had managed to reach the far side of the road. Several straggled behind.

Kassan slammed on the brakes. As the twins braced themselves against the back of their seats, the car skidded across the road. It headed for the edge of a steep drop-off.

# CHAPTER X

## A SHOWER OF SHOES

WHEN the car finally stopped, everyone was too frightened to move. Finally Kassan edged out of his seat onto the road. He surveyed the situation.

"Whew!" Nan shivered. "That was awfully close!"

"We're okay," Kassan said in a relieved tone. "All you get out this side and I back into the middle of road." Terry led the younger children away while Bert directed Kassan. All this time the sheep had been milling around the car and the children.

Suddenly a shout came from up the hill and a ragged young man ran down the road. His torn robe was tucked up around his waist, and he wore dilapidated sandals on his bare feet.

The shepherd shook his long staff in Kassan's face and talked rapidly in Arabic. Kassan replied in equally loud tones, spreading out his arms in a gesture of helplessness.

"Goodness!" Terry cried. "What are they saying?"

"Shepherd say we hurt his sheep," Ali translated. "Kassan say sheep almost cause us to be killed!"

Terry opened her purse and took out some money. "Here, Ali," she said. "I suppose the sheep were as frightened as we were. Give this to the shepherd and tell him we're sorry."

Ali handed the money to the young man and said a few words to him. Immediately the shepherd stopped yelling. He turned toward Terry and made a deep bow. Then he raised his staff and began to drive the sheep to the side of the road.

Kassan threw up his hands again in a gesture of despair and opened the car doors for Terry and the children. In a few minutes, with a wave to the sheepherder, they were on their way to Damascus once more.

There was no sign of the gray American car as they drove into the city. "We'd better go straight to the bazaar," Bert suggested. "That's probably where Omir went."

Kassan shook his head. "Streets around bazaar too narrow for me to drive car," he remarked. "I park, then show you where bazaar is."

"I want something to eat first!" Freddie insisted.

"Yes," said Terry. "I think we should all have some lunch before we do anything else."

The others agreed, and Kassan found a small clean-looking restaurant in the suburbs of the city. It was past the regular meal time so they were served quickly.

"This is yummy!" Flossie said, tasting the dish of rice and lamb which was put before her.

The meal ended with a bowl of delicious fresh fruit. After eating it the children declared themselves ready to continue the search for Omir.

"Is the bazaar a large store?" Nan asked.

Kassan laughed. "Is many stores. You find out."

When they reached the center of the city, the children could see how difficult it was to drive. The streets were narrow and jammed with cars, buses, trucks, and horse-drawn carts.

Finally Kassan found a place to leave his automobile and motioned the others to follow him. He led them to the opening of a narrow lane which was lined with small shops. A slatted roof stretched from one side of the street to the other, shutting out most of the sunlight.

"This is one entrance to bazaar," Kassan explained. "I not like to leave car alone. I go now. When you ready to leave, ask boy to bring you to

Bank of Syria. I meet you there." He pointed to a large building nearby.

Terry nodded and followed the children into the narrow street. Most of the shops were open in front and not more than eight feet wide. They were filled with things to sell—jewelry, brass work, clothing, and food.

The roadway was teaming with people walking or riding donkeys. Some of the men wore western dress, but most of the natives had on long gowns and white head coverings. The few women were in black with black veils over their heads and faces.

"I wonder how they can see," Nan thought as she turned to look at several of the black-robed figures. She was just passing a shoe store. Long strings of gold and silver brocade slippers dangled on each side of the entrance.

All at once there was a sound of "Eech! Eech-ah!"

Nan looked up to see a donkey break away from the man who was leading it and gallop down the street toward her. Quickly she jumped back into the shop to avoid the runaway.

Her foot slipped, and she grabbed the string of shoes to steady herself. The next second the string broke, and Nan was buried under a shower of shoes!

"Oh!" she cried. "Help!"

Terry and the other children heard her. They

"Oh!" Nan cried. "Help!"

ran back and helped Nan up. All of them began to collect the slippers.

"I'm so sorry!" Nan told the shopkeeper who hurried in from another shop where he had been visiting.

"It is nothing," the man insisted. "I can put them up again. I would like to offer you a cold drink and some food. Please!"

Terry hesitated, but Ali assured her this was the custom in the East and the man would be offended if they refused. She consented and he gave the visitors chunks of bread.

"This is like bread at mission," Ali said.

As the twins swallowed the dry pieces, they began to cough.

Ali grinned. "Many year ago when man not swallow bread easy, he not true man," he said.

Bert whispered, "They can have it. This bread is just plain stale!"

Nevertheless, the Bobbseys and Terry politely finished their portions and sipped the delicious fruit drinks from paper cups.

Then Nan said, "I'd like to buy a pair of bedroom slippers."

"I will get them," the shop owner said.

Nan, Flossie, and Terry tried on the beautiful slippers and made their choices. Flossie insisted upon bright red ones with a camel design on each toe.

Meanwhile Bert asked the owner, "Do you

know where a man named Attiyah has his shop?"

"Does he sell shoes?"

Bert admitted that he did not know but explained that they were trying to find a man named Omir who worked for Mr. Attiyah. The shopkeeper shrugged.

"That is a common name in the bazaar," he declared. "But if you go to the end of this street and turn right there is an Attiyah who owns an antique shop. But don't buy from him. He has a bad reputation."

Terry thanked the man for his kindness and they all started down the street again.

"Goodness," said Nan, "it would be easy to get lost in here!" She looked around at the maze of alleys leading off in all directions.

A few minutes later Flossie ran back to her sister. "Freddie's lost! He was right beside me and now I can't find him anywhere!" A tear began to roll down Flossie's pink cheek.

"Don't worry. He can't be far away," Nan assured her.

Hand in hand, Nan and Flossie retraced their steps, peering into shops on both sides. There was no sign of Freddie. While passing an archway which led into a courtyard, they heard some women laughing.

"I wonder what's going on in there?" Nan said curiously.

"Let's see!" Flossie ran through the archway, and Nan followed. They stopped, surprised at the scene before them.

The courtyard was surrounded on all sides by old buildings which seemed to be apartments. In the center was a well. A group of women were filling large jugs with water from it and in the midst of them, helping, was the lost Bobbsey twin!

"Freddie, why did you leave us?" Nan called.

"I saw the ladies pulling up the water bucket and I decided to help," Freddie explained. "They were glad to have me!" The women nodded pleasantly and walked away with the water jars balanced on their heads.

Terry, Bert, and Ali were waiting for Nan and the small twins at the next corner. Together they walked along the street looking for Attiyah's shop. They reached the end without finding it.

Ali stopped a boy pushing a cart loaded with fruit and asked about Mr. Attiyah. The lad thought a moment, then pointed down an alleyway.

"I guess we turned the wrong way," Bert said.

"I'm so mixed up now, I don't know which way we came," Nan admitted.

They turned down the alleyway looking for

the antique shop but could not find it. The street came to a dead end at the entrance to a mosque. Through the wide door the children could see into the courtyard.

"There's a policeman," Bert reported. "I'm going to ask him about Attiyah's shop."

"What did he say?" Freddie asked when Bert returned.

"We're on the wrong street. It's the next one up here." Bert started back the way they had come, followed by the others.

A short time later he turned down another narrow lane, then stopped abruptly. He motioned the rest to run back around the corner.

"What is the matter?" Ali asked when Bert joined them.

"Our mystery man, Omir, is standing in front of the shop on the other side of that street. And he has the toy camel with him! The shop seems to be closed."

"I think you should get that policeman, Bert," Terry said firmly. "We'll wait here for you."

"But Omir might go away in the meantime," Bert objected.

"He is not so apt to recognize Ali," Nan suggested. "He can watch Omir from the shop across the street and warn us if the thief starts to leave."

Bert agreed reluctantly and ran back toward

the mosque. Ali slipped around the corner and took up his post in a rug shop. Terry, Nan, and the small twins pretended to look at the jewelry displayed in a shop window nearby.

In a few minutes Ali returned. "Owner come back to shop and Omir go inside with him," he reported.

"Oh dear!" said Nan. "Where are Bert and the policeman?"

"Here they come!" Freddie told her.

Bert and the officer hurried around the corner toward Attiyah's shop. The others ran after them. A moment later the pursuers burst into the antique shop.

Omir stood beside a heavy carved table with the toy camel in one hand. In the other he held a knife ready to cut into the stuffed animal!

"Stop!" Flossie shrieked.

Omir turned, startled. When he saw the policeman, he began to run toward the back of the shop!

"Halt!" the officer ordered.

# CHAPTER XI

## FIRST FLIGHT

THE policeman hurried to Omir's side and took the toy camel from his hand. Without another word he seized the man's knife and cut a gash in the back of the stuffed animal.

Omir and Attiyah watched intently with Terry and the children as the policeman pulled the stuffing from the toy. There was nothing hidden inside!

After a second of silence, Omir burst out, "Why you do this? I bring a present from Egypt for my friend's son and you destroy it! Why?"

All this time the shop owner, Attiyah, had not said a word. Now he joined in Omir's protests. He acted very angry.

The policeman interrupted him. "These American children said you had a valuable Egyptian antique hidden in the camel. I see they were mistaken."

He motioned the twins to follow him from

the shop. Outside, he cautioned them against accusing people falsely and stalked away.

"Omir didn't have the little horse in the camel!" Flossie wailed as the travelers started back up the street.

Bert shook his head, bewildered. "I can't understand it. Why would Halif give him a toy camel if it didn't hide something? And why was Omir trying to get away from us if he isn't guilty?"

Nan spoke up. "I was watching Omir and Attiyah when the policeman opened that camel. I'm sure Omir was as surprised as we were when there was nothing inside it. And Attiyah looked furious!"

"You think—"

At that moment Ali ran up. He was excited.

"What has happened, Ali?" Terry asked.

Ali explained that when the others had followed the policeman away from Attiyah's shop, he had slipped into the next doorway.

"Omir and Attiyah shout in Arabic and I want to hear what they say."

The twins begged Ali to go on. He told them that Attiyah had been very angry with Omir.

"Then Omir tell him Halif is a-a-what you call—a double-crosser!"

"So the antique horse *was* supposed to be in the toy camel!" Nan declared.

"Yes," Ali said. "Attiyah say Halif must still have horse. He order Omir to fly back to Cairo and get it! Attiyah come to Cairo soon as he find someone to watch shop."

"Then we must find Halif before Omir does!" Bert cried. "How can we get to Cairo fast?"

"We'll ask Kassan!" Terry was as excited as the children. She began to walk rapidly down the street.

"Come on!" Flossie called to the others. "Terry knows the way."

A short time later the group came from the dim streets of the bazaar into bright sunlight. Nan looked around. "I don't see Kassan or the Bank of Syria," she said.

"Oh dear!" Terry groaned. "I'm afraid I led you out the wrong way. This isn't the entrance we came in!"

Ali stopped a passerby and asked directions. "It not far from here," the boy assured Terry. "Just two block up and turn right."

"We'll have to hurry!" Nan started off at a brisk pace followed by the others. When she reached the second corner, she stopped uncertainly. "Is this where we turn, Ali?"

The little Egyptian boy was not with them! Surprised, the children looked around. On the other side of the street they noticed a large vacant lot. In the center were many camels. Some were standing, some lying down. They were being loaded with cartons of merchandise by a group of men in native dress.

Suddenly there was a great commotion. The camels began to bellow and move about uneasily. Then came the crunching sound of paper cartons being trampled.

The loaders shouted at the camels. In a second a crowd had gathered to watch. The camel drivers pulled at the reins in an effort to control the animals, which appeared about to stampede. The onlookers shouted words of advice or encouragement.

At the height of the confusion, the twins saw a boy crawl out from among the robed natives. He ran across the street.

*Ali!*

The boy motioned them to follow as he dashed down the street toward the bank building in the distance. When they were out of sight of the crowd, he slowed down.

"Ali! For Pete's sake, what—" Bert cried.

"I think I see Farah!" the Egyptian boy exclaimed. "But when I run up to camels, they get frightened. Run away."

Ali went on to tell the Bobbseys that camels are unpredictable, nervous animals, and easily upset. "When they step on cartons, I think I better go. And anyway," he added sheepishly, "my Farah not there!"

The twins saw a boy crawl out from among the robed natives

By this time the group had reached Kassan and the car. Quickly Bert told the driver that they wanted to get to Cairo as soon as possible.

Kassan looked at his watch. "There is plane to Cairo at four o'clock," he said. "You have time for refreshment. Then I drive you to airport."

He led them to an amusing little restaurant with pictures on the walls of Egyptian clowns with elephants and a moonlight scene on the desert with dancing white mice.

Flossie giggled, "I love mice."

"We think they bring us luck," said Kassan.

On another wall were cats of all ages and breeds. "I guess you like pussycats in your country," Flossie said to Kassan.

He smiled. "Yes. You see, thousand year ago in ancient Egypt, there was goddess of joy and wisdom. She appear in desert country in form of cat. Temple built for all cats of village. When they die, they made into mummies like the queen and put in temple to honor goddess."

The Bobbseys enjoyed the story and wanted to hear more, but Terry said, "It's getting late. We'd better drive to the airport."

When they stopped in front of the main building there, Bert jumped out. "I'll buy the tickets and meet you at the gate," he offered. Terry gave him the money and he dashed off.

Kassan carried the bags into the building, then said good-by. "I hope you catch thief," he said, smiling and shaking hands with each of the children.

Bert hurried up. "The plane is leaving in one minute," he reported. "Hurry, everybody! Good-by, Kassan."

With a wave to the kindly driver, Terry, Ali, and the twins hurried out through the gate. As soon as they had taken their seats, the doors were closed and the plane began to move.

"Look!" Bert said to Nan, pointing back toward the departure building. "Attiyah's at the gate! He seems to be arguing, but they're not letting him through!"

"Good!" Nan sat back in her seat. "Now if we can only find Halif before he gets to Cairo!"

The big plane taxied to the end of the runway. It swung around and waited for the signal to take off. Then the engine began to roar and the aircraft sped down the concrete path.

Bert looked across the aisle where Ali was seated with Terry. His hands gripped the seat arms tightly, and he sat stiffly against the back of the chair. He looked frightened.

"Haven't you ever flown before?" Bert asked him.

Ali shook his head and kept his lips pressed tightly together. He did not look at Bert but fixed his gaze on the door leading to the cockpit of the plane.

"Don't worry," Nan called to him. "When we

get in the air, you won't even know we're moving."

Ali still looked unconvinced but said nothing. A few minutes later they were airborne. As soon as the "Fasten Seat Belts" sign went off, Freddie and Flossie jumped up and raced down the aisle past Ali and Terry.

"Please sit down," Ali begged, reaching out and grabbing Freddie's arm. "You will upset plane!"

Freddie and Flossie giggled, but Terry put her hand on Ali's. "There's no danger of that," she said kindly. "The plane is perfectly safe. Try to enjoy the flight."

Ali smiled a little, but he stared straight in front of him until the plane began its descent at Cairo. Nothing any of the children said made him relax.

"I guess Ali just doesn't like being a bird," Flossie observed with a sigh.

It was growing dark by the time the plane landed at the Cairo airport. "I'll phone Uncle Abdel and tell him we're here," Bert offered. He returned in a few minutes.

"Uncle Abdel was surprised to hear we're back," Bert told the others. "He is sending a car to pick us up."

"I go home on bus," Ali declared. "Thank you for take me with you. I come to see you soon."

With a wave and a wide smile he hurried off.

"But—" Bert began. He was too late. Ali was already boarding a city bus.

"I thought Ali was going to help us find Halif," Flossie remarked. "And now he's gone away!"

"Never mind," Terry said. "I'm sure you'll see him again."

The Bobbseys and Terry did not have to wait long before Uncle Abdel's car drew up at the airport building.

"Mr. Gouda is holding dinner for you," the chauffeur informed them as they drove toward the city.

There was an excited reunion when the twins ran into the house. Danny and Tom were in the hall to meet them. "Did you get the antique horse?" Tom asked eagerly.

Terry spoke up. "You can tell your story at the table," she said. "I think you should all get ready for dinner at once."

But later at the table there was no stopping the Bobbseys. They told of their stay in Alexandria and of following Omir onto the ship to Beirut and then to Damascus.

"And we almost ran into a lot of sheep," Freddie said.

"Freddie got lost in the bazaar," Flossie added.

"And Ali thought he saw Farah," Nan put in.

"Well, you Bobbseys are extraordinary detectives," Uncle Abdel commented admiringly.

Danny grunted. "I don't think they're so good. They didn't find the horse. *I* have a really good clue to it!"

# CHAPTER XII

## DANNY OVERBOARD

"YOU have?" Nan cried. "What is it? Tell us!"

After pleas from the twins, Danny was persuaded to tell the others what he meant.

"While you Bobbseys were away," he said, "I did some detective work myself. I walked down to the Nile River. It isn't far from here."

Danny told them that at the river he had made friends with an Egyptian who owned a sailboat. "They call them *feluccas*," the boy said loftily.

"Well, get on with your clue," Bert urged.

Danny scowled, but continued. "I told this man—his name is Gamal—about the person you're trying to find."

"Well?" Nan inquired.

"Gamal knows where Halif lives!" Danny declared triumphantly.

"He does?"

"Where?"

"Can we go there?"

The questions came thick and fast. Danny told the twins that his friend Gamal took cargoes up and down the river in his felucca. While at work he had become acquainted with Halif and often visited him.

"I asked Gamal," Danny went on, "if he would take some of us to see Halif, and he said he would."

"That's wonderful, Danny!" Nan cried. She turned to Tom. "May we go?"

Tom looked uncertain. "I don't think you should go alone with this man," he replied. "Can your friend take all of us, Danny?"

The boy nodded.

Uncle Abdel spoke up. "I have a friend who knows all the felucca owners. I'll ask him about this Gamal."

After dinner Mr. Gouda telephoned his friend. Then he said to Tom, "I think it will be all right. My friend says Gamal's a very trustworthy man and you should have no fears about letting the children go out with him."

"Goody!" Flossie cried. "We're going sailing!" The Bobbseys lived near Lake Metoka in Lakeport and loved to sail on the lake.

Very early the next morning Tom drove Danny and the Bobbseys down to the river dock. Gamal was waiting for them. He was a young man with twinkling brown eyes. His galabia and turban were shining clean.

The felucca was a wide, one-masted craft which sat low in the water. A herd of goats to be delivered up the river milled about on the foredeck.

Freddie grinned. "It'll be fun sailing with goats!" he declared.

Bert's eyes were on the strange-looking boat. "What a high sail!" he exclaimed.

Gamal explained that to catch the slightest breeze on the river the feluccas were built so that the yard could stretch the mainsail to a height more than twice that of the mast.

"The feluccas are lovely!" Nan said as she watched the graceful sailboats skimming up and down the river. "They look like moths!"

Uncle Abdel's cook had packed a picnic lunch for the children. Bert and Danny carried it from the car and stowed it away under Gamal's direction. They said good-by to Tom, and Gamal cast off.

"Good luck! See you this evening!" the counselor called.

The goats bleated loudly while the children waved from the deck and the felucca began its journey up the Nile. When the buildings of Cairo had faded into the distance, the Bobbseys watched the countryside slide by. The river wound between small green fields, dark patches of plowed ground and clumps of date palms.

"We can grow crops only where we get water from river," Gamal explained. "We have very little rain in Egypt."

After a while Danny grew restless. He got up and walked forward. A rope was stretched across the deck to keep the goats from wandering around the boat. Danny stood looking at them. An old nanny goat tossed her head and bleated.

*Maa—maa!*

"Maa yourself. Maybe you're hungry," Danny said. "They say goats will eat anything. I'll find out."

He looked around for something to feed the goat. His eye fell on a piece of torn sailcloth. Carrying it in his hand, Danny stepped over the rope and held out the cloth to the animal.

Another goat had been watching Danny suspiciously. When it saw the boy turn around, the goat backed up a few steps, then charged forward.

*Danny went sailing through the air and landed with a loud splash in the river!*

Freddie jumped up and ran to the side of the felucca. "Man overboard!" he shouted, pointing to Danny, who had bobbed to the surface and was treading water.

Quickly Gamal seized a pole and held it out to the boy. In another minute an angry Danny Rugg was pulled aboard.

Danny landed with a loud splash in the river!

"That mean old goat butted me and I wasn't doing anything to him!" the boy sputtered.

"I regret it," Gamal said politely. "But you not hurt and sun soon dry your clothes."

"Why don't we eat our lunch now?" Nan spoke up quickly to change the subject.

"Yes!" Freddie and Flossie agreed at once.

Bert brought the picnic basket, and Nan spread out the sandwiches and fruit on a paper tablecloth. Gamal smilingly refused a sandwich and opened his little package of cold rice. They all ate hungrily.

"We stop at next village to deliver some of goats," Gamal announced when the remains of the lunch had been put back into the basket. A short time later he turned the bow into the bank where a few mud-brick houses were clustered in a small grove of date palms.

Several men hurried to the boat and helped Gamal unload a few of the goats. The children watched interestedly.

"Look at the little girl leading that big, funny-looking cow!" Flossie exclaimed.

"That's a water buffalo, silly!" Danny jeered, proud of his knowledge. "They use them in Egypt for plowing fields, don't they, Gamal?"

The boatman nodded. "Yes. Little girl take care of family buffalo."

Flossie watched the child as she held the animal's rope while he drank from the river. She was dressed in a long black dress and wore a black shawl over her head and shoulders.

"I'm going to talk to her!" Flossie jumped to the bank and ran over to the Egyptian child.

Fortunately the little girl spoke English, and soon they were chatting busily. Nan noticed Flossie take off the bright cotton triangle which she wore over her yellow curls and hold it out to the black-robed girl.

The child shook her head violently and backed away from Flossie. Then they both giggled. With a friendly wave Flossie ran back to the felucca.

"I wanted to trade hats," she explained, "but the girl said no. I guess her mommy wouldn't have liked it." Flossie sighed.

By this time the goats for the village had been unloaded, and Gamal cast off once more.

"When are we going to find Halif?" Bert asked.

"In next village," Gamal replied. "That's where rest of goats go."

There was very little wind as the felucca swung out into the middle of the river. Gamal looked up at the yard. "We have to give her more sail," he observed. "You hold tiller while I go up?"

"I will!" Freddie offered.

With a quick motion Gamal pulled his galabia between his legs and grasped the hem in his teeth. The next minute he was scrambling up the slender yard like a monkey. A few quick motions, and the sail billowed out to its fullest.

Freddie was so fascinated in watching the boatman that he forgot the tiller. A sudden current caught the craft and turned it toward the shore.

"Freddie!" Bert yelled, dashing over to his brother.

Quickly Freddie righted the boat and steered to the middle of the river once more.

"I'm sorry," Freddie apologized as Gamal reached the deck.

"No harm done," he said cheerfully, taking charge of the tiller once more. He looked up at his billowing sail proudly. "Now we make better time."

With the added sail the *felucca* did move more quickly, and before long the children could see another mud-hut village in the distance.

"We almost there," Gamal told them. "I bring goats to market they hold today. I think man you seek there."

"That's great!" Bert replied.

Danny added, "I hope he still has Uncle Abdel's toy horse!"

Gamal looked surprised but he busied himself with bringing the felucca in toward the river bank. When the boat was safely tied up, Nan and Flossie jumped ashore. The boys helped Gamal herd the goats down a plank. As soon as they were on shore the boatman directed the boys to drive the animals through the village.

"Market is on other side of town," he explained.

The natives came running from all directions to see the strange children helping with the goats. The little Egyptian boys and girls giggled when Freddie and Flossie waved at them.

At a short distance some other boys and girls were playing tug-of-war with a long black rope.

"Come on!" Freddie motioned to his sister. "Let's play too!"

The twins bounded toward the group. Freddie ran to one end of the line and grabbed the rope while Flossie skipped to the other side and held on.

One little Egyptian boy who was on the rival team tried to step on the rope but all he succeeded in doing was to topple into a somersault underneath it. Everyone laughed.

Freddie's team lost the match. But Flossie said, "It was fun, anyway."

Terry called the younger twins back to the boat. They climbed into the felucca and set off. Finally the last of the huts was left behind.

"There is the market," Gamal said.

Inside a roped-off enclosure the Bobbseys and Danny saw a busy scene. Goats, camels, and water buffaloes milled about. Egyptians in long gowns and turbans were bargaining loudly.

"But where is Halif?" Nan asked eagerly, searching the faces of the men.

Gamal pointed.

# CHAPTER XIII

## EXPLODING RICE

"OH dear," Nan cried, as the boatman waved to a short, fat young man. "He's the wrong Halif!"

Freddie turned to Danny Rugg. "You're mean!"

"I think you're horrid!" Flossie joined in.

"Aw," said Danny, "I just wanted to help solve the mystery!"

"Well, why didn't you find out first what Halif looked like?" Bert asked. "We've lost a whole day when we could have been looking for him in Cairo."

Danny winced. "I made a mistake."

Nan was more understanding. "You couldn't help it, Danny."

Gamal had been listening to the children. Now he spoke up. "My friend is not the man you seek?" he asked.

"No." Nan described the tall, white-bearded

119

Halif and told the boatman why they wanted to find him. "Do you know this Halif?"

Gamal shook his head. "I am sorry I cannot help you."

"When are we ever going to find the horse?" Flossie piped up.

The children strolled around the market until the boatman had finished his business. Then he led them back to the river.

"We will make good time to Cairo," the boatman declared. "The wind is from the south and will blow us down the river." He smiled. "Then you find right Halif."

Gamal was right about the wind. It filled the giant sail and the felucca sped homeward.

Tom was standing on the dock when Gamal tied up. "Any luck?" he called.

The twins waited until they had thanked Gamal and said good-by to him before they told Tom the story of their disappointment.

"That's too bad," the counselor remarked. "But cheer up. I might have a clue for you." He grinned. "I heard today that a man named Salah works in the kitchen of the King Tut Hotel."

"Uncle Abdel's missing servant?" Bert exclaimed.

The twins were excited all over again. Salah could tell them where the antique toy horse was!

After dinner Nan said she thought they should still try to find Halif too.

"Maybe the police have some news of him," Bert suggested. "I'll phone them."

He had a long conversation with the chief. The others waited impatiently to hear what the mamour had to say. When Bert came back, his face was glum.

"What did he say?" Nan asked.

"The police haven't seen Halif. I told the mamour about our trip to Damascus and what happened there. He promised to be on the lookout for Omir too."

"The police haven't any clues to Salah either?" Nan inquired.

"No."

"Why don't we go to the hotel?" Freddie suggested.

"That's a good idea." Bert agreed.

"But not until tomorrow," Terry said firmly.

The next morning it was decided that only the older Bobbsey twins would look for Salah. Uncle Abdel had to go to Alexandria for the day so Tom drove Nan and Bert to the King Tut Hotel. "I'll wait for you in the parking lot," he said.

The two children walked into the lobby. It was filled with tourists and dragomen. The men behind the desk were busy assigning rooms and answering questions. No one paid any attention to the twins.

"Let's go right to the kitchen," Nan urged. Through an open door they could see a large dining room. The tables were set, but the room was empty at this hour. At the far end were several swinging doors.

"Okay," Bert agreed.

The twins walked through the dining room into the kitchen beyond. It was large, with a marble floor and whitewashed walls. Along one side stood a long range. A short, fat man stood before it. He wore a white apron over his caftan and a high white chef's hat perched sideways on his head. He had just taken the cover off a big pot of boiling water.

"Let's ask him about Salah," Bert said, and they walked over. The cook had his back to them.

"Pardon me," Bert began just as the man picked up a bowl of uncooked rice and started to pour it into the water. "Can you tell us—"

The chef jumped at the unexpected voice. He turned toward Bert and without looking continued to pour the rice into the boiling water.

A moment later, Nan yelled, "Look out! It's exploding!"

She was too late. The large amount of rice had

"Look out!" Nan yelled. "It's exploding!"

already started to boil over. Rice flew in every direction, covering the floor with the hot, gooey liquid.

*"Eeah!"* the chef screamed, jumping back. He looked angry and began talking fast in Arabic.

Two kitchen workers rushed up with mops and hastily began to clean the floor. The cook shook his fist at Bert. "Look what you do to me! Get out of my kitchen!"

"We're sorry." Nan tried to soothe the angry man. "We're looking for someone named Salah. We think he works here."

"No one named Salah here!" The cook waved his arm in dismissal.

When the twins reached the lobby, Nan began to giggle. "I never saw exploding rice before!"

When they returned to Uncle Abdel's house, Freddie burst out, "Mr. Mallakh telephoned. He thinks he knows where Halif is!"

"Where?"

Danny answered. "Mr. Mallakh thought that since Halif works at archaeological digs sometimes, maybe he went out to one they're working at now on the desert east of Cairo."

"Do you suppose we'd be allowed to go to the dig?" Bert inquired.

"Yes. Mr. Mallakh is going out there tomorrow and he said he'd take us all along. He says we may ask Ali to come with us."

Freddie was jumping up and down. "And we can go on camels!" he shouted excitedly.

"That's keen!" Bert cried.

Tom put an arm around the little boy. "Not so fast, sonny. The invitation was only for the older children. I'm sorry."

"Oh phooey!" said Freddie.

"I'm not going," Tom told him. "We'll have fun together here." He told the others that Terry would ride with them.

"How will we find Ali?" Bert asked suddenly. "Does anybody know where he lives?"

The children looked at one another in dismay. "Uncle Abdel will know," Nan said. "Ali told him the name of the street he lives on when we called from Alexandria."

"But Uncle Abdel won't be back until tonight and we want to ask Ali now!" Danny pointed out.

"His father is a brass worker," Nan remarked. "And I remember Ali said most of the brass workers live on the same street. Perhaps we can find it."

"It's probably in the Musky," said Terry. "That's a street of bazaars here in Cairo. If we go there, maybe we'll see Ali."

"Okay," Tom agreed. "You take the older children to the Musky while Freddie, Flossie, and I make some plans for tomorrow." He winked at the younger twins.

"I'd rather go to the river and talk to Gamal," Danny objected.

"Okay."

After lunch in the cool dining room of Uncle Abdel's house, Danny set off for the river while Terry and the older twins drove to the Musky section of the city. Terry parked the car, then she and the children set out on foot through the narrow, winding streets.

"Look at all the jewelry!" Nan exclaimed, pausing to glance into a shop window filled with gold chains, bracelets, and rings.

"These stores all seem to carry jewelry," Bert observed. "Ali's father can't be here."

The group turned down another narrow alley. Here they found shops where pottery was sold. The next street was full of tailoring shops.

"Where's the brass?" Nan asked.

"Down there," Terry called. She pointed into another lane. On both sides of the narrow passage hung pots and pans, trays and bowls of shining copper and brass.

The counselor and the twins hurried along the street, peering on either side for a glimpse of their little Egyptian friend.

"Here he is!" Nan finally called out.

Ali was crouched in the doorway of a shop. He held a large copper tray between his knees and was carefully pounding silver wires into grooves which had been cut into the copper. Ali started at the sound of Nan's voice.

"Welcome!" he cried, jumping up and bowing low. "I welcome you to my father's house!"

"Hi, Ali!" Bert said. "We're glad we found you. We want you to come out to an archaeological dig with us tomorrow."

Ali hung his head. "My father angry with me for run away to Alexandria. I must stay home and work on copper."

"Oh, Ali!" Nan protested. "You must come with us. We're going to ride on camels. Perhaps you can find your Farah!"

At this moment a smiling Egyptian came to the doorway. "You are Ali's American friends?" he asked in a pleasant voice. "Will you enter my house?" He stood aside for Terry and the Bobbseys to step into the shop.

Ali ran past them into a room at the back. In a second he returned. "My brothers and sisters!" he announced proudly.

Seven Egyptian children, all younger than Ali, stepped shyly through the curtains which separated the shop from the rest of the house. The youngest, a girl, could only toddle.

When all the introductions had been made, Terry explained their errand. Ali's father looked stern and shook his head.

"Ali must stay home in punishment for running away."

"But—" Nan began.

The Egyptian shook his head, and the twins felt it would be useless to argue with the man. They moved toward the door to leave.

In the distance came the sound of a motorcycle. It turned down the narrow street of the brass workers. As the visitors waited for it to pass, Ali's baby sister suddenly toddled into the street directly in the path of the speeding motorcycle!

Instantly Nan dashed from the shop, and snatched the child up in her arms. The motorcycle roared past!

# CHAPTER XIV

## A MYSTERIOUS PROWLER

"MY baby!" Ali's father ran to Nan and grabbed the child. He covered her with kisses. Then when he had set her down again in the shop he turned to Nan.

"You saved my little girl," he said solemnly. "What I do to repay you?"

Nan was embarrassed. "I just happened to be the person nearest the street," she said.

"But I must do something for you," the shop owner insisted.

Nan smiled. "Then would you let Ali come with us tomorrow?"

The Egyptian smiled. "So be it," he said. "My son go with you."

"Oh, thank you!" Nan cried.

Ali looked delighted. Bert clapped him on the back gleefully. All the children began to make plans for the next day. It was decided that Ali would meet Terry, Bert, Nan, and Danny at the edge of the city where Mr. Mallakh had told them they would find the camels.

"I hope we'll catch Halif this time," Bert remarked on the way back to Uncle Abdel's.

"And find poor Salah!" Nan looked worried. "I wonder if he is in trouble!"

Uncle Abdel had returned from Alexandria and greeted the children when they came to dinner. He was interested to hear of the proposed trip into the desert.

"I am glad you will have the chance to see a real dig," he said. "And I also hope you find a clue to the antique horse."

After dinner their host led the two counselors and the children into the parlor. "I bought something in Alexandria today," he explained, "to add to my collection. Perhaps you would like to see it?"

"Yes, please," Flossie piped up. "Is it another little animal?"

Uncle Abdel smiled at her. "Not this time. It is something very beautiful, and it came from an ancient tomb."

The children watched as he opened one of the doors of the wall cabinet and took out a vase about eight inches high.

"It is made of alabaster," Uncle Abdel explained. "Look!" He held a lighted candle behind the graceful vase.

"Oh!" Nan gasped. "You can see right

through it, and the vase never got broken!"

The flickering light of the candle filtered through the fragile marble-like material and revealed a delicate design of flowers etched into the vase.

"It's beautiful," Terry commented.

Uncle Abdel explained that in ancient Egypt, whenever a wealthy man was buried, all the things that he might need in an afterlife were put into his tomb with him. "It is from these tombs that our Egyptian treasures have come," he told them.

A slight movement outside the open window made Bert turn his head. He was just in time to see something white slide past. It looked like a kuffiyah.

"That's funny," Bert thought. "Was someone listening at the window?" Then he decided that it must have been his imagination, and he would say nothing about it.

As Uncle Abdel replaced the vase in the cabinet and locked the door, Danny said, "Your collection is worth a lot of money, isn't it?"

Mr. Gouda nodded. "That is why I keep it locked up at night."

Because of the trip planned for the next day the older children went to bed at the same time as Freddie and Flossie.

Nan tossed about for a while, then fell asleep. She was dreaming that the camel she was riding suddenly began to sing. She awoke laughing, but then sat up in bed a little frightened. Had she heard a noise?

She looked over at Flossie, but the small girl was sleeping quietly. Nan listened intently. She heard a slight tapping sound.

Grabbing robe and slippers, Nan crept out into the large center hall. At the top of the stairs she met Bert.

"Did you hear something too?" he asked his twin in a whisper.

"Yes," Nan answered. "I think there's some-one downstairs!"

A faint light from the street came through the glass of the wide front door. The twins crept quietly down the carpeted stairs. They stopped in the hall and listened again.

"It's from the parlor," Bert declared when another faint tapping sound reached their ears.

Opening the parlor door quickly, Bert stopped. A short, heavy-set figure in a long robe and kuffiyah stood in front of the cabinet at the end of the room. By the light of a small flash he was trying to pry open the carved door!

Bert motioned to Nan to follow him as he made his way silently toward the man. The next second there was a *splash!*

Bert, with Nan close behind him, had stumbled into the shallow pool in the center of

Bert motioned Nan to follow him

the room! The mysterious figure at the cabinet had heard the splash. He quickly put out the flashlight and ran from the room. The twins heard the click of the front door.

"Oh dear!" Nan exclaimed. "We almost caught him!"

"That was Omir!" Bert cried, picking himself up and holding out a hand to Nan. "I saw that brass tassel on his wrist just before I fell!"

Nan began to giggle. "I'll bet we really scared him!"

At that moment the lights in the room came on. Uncle Abdel stood in the doorway. "What's the matter? I heard a noise down here!"

Bert and Nan explained about the intruder. Uncle Abdel rushed over to the cabinet and tried the door. It was still locked.

"That's good!" he exclaimed. "Evidently you two frightened the thief away before he could open the cabinet. Thank you."

"We think we know who the thief is," Bert declared. He told Uncle Abdel about seeing the figure in the kuffiyah at the window earlier in the evening. "I'm sure he was Omir, the man we followed to Damascus!"

"I'll notify the police at once!" Uncle Abdel hurried to the telephone.

The next morning at breakfast the other children were amazed when Bert told them of the happenings during the night.

"You Bobbseys always have all the excitement!" Danny complained. "I didn't hear a thing!"

"You shouldn't sleep so soundly!" Bert teased. "You'll never learn to be a detective that way." Danny scowled at him and went on eating.

Tom drove Terry and the three older children to the camel stable. Mr. Mallakh and Ali were waiting for them.

"We each have a camel to ride," the archaeologist explained. "There are three other beasts to carry our camping equipment."

The camel assigned to Bert appeared restless. It shifted from one foot to another, stretched its neck into the air and grunted continually.

Bert noticed a bundle of greens lashed to each of the camels' saddles. "What's that stuff?" he asked curiously.

"It clover," Ali replied. "Each camel carry own food every day."

"All aboard!" Mr. Mallakh called out. The stable attendants ordered the camels to their knees and the group mounted.

With the archaeologist leading the way, the procession started off single file. Before long they were plodding across the sandy desert.

"Isn't this fun?" Nan called back to Bert. "We're a real desert caravan!"

When they had ridden about two hours under the hot sun, the party reached a small oasis. Mr. Mallakh called a halt.

"We'll rest here for a minute," he said, slipping off as his camel knelt in the sand. The others followed, and all headed for a cluster of palm trees which provided welcome shade.

Ali produced a flask of cold water and paper cups. Everyone drank thirstily.

"How about the camels?" Danny asked.

"They go all day without a drink," Mr. Mallakh replied. Then he added, "We were lucky this oasis didn't prove to be a mirage. They have caused the death of many men."

"What's a mirage?" Danny asked.

The archaeologist said it happened when one's eyes played tricks. "A traveler on the desert may think he sees an oasis, or a mountain or even a ship ahead of him in the sand. He keeps trying to reach the spot and often becomes hopelessly lost!"

Danny shuddered. "I don't want to get lost."

Bert laughed. "I'd like to see a mirage."

"It's an interesting sight if you can just remember that it is only a mirage," Mr. Mallakh said.

By this time the travelers were rested. They mounted the kneeling camels and the procession started off once more.

The pause seemed to have made Bert's camel more restless than ever. The beast turned its long neck back in an effort to reach the green clover on the saddle.

"Stop that!" Bert jerked the reins sharply and brought the camel's head around.

The animal tossed its head into the air and gave a high cry. At the sound Ali turned and rode toward Bert. He jerked the reins again. The camel twisted suddenly and grabbed a bunch of clover from the saddle.

The quick movement unseated Bert. His feet flew into the air and he landed with a *thump* on the sand!

# CHAPTER XV

### VANISHING LADDER

EMBARRASSED at his fall, Bert got to his feet quickly. He grinned sheepishly at Ali when the Egyptian boy rode up. "I guess I'm not a very good camel rider."

"You okay?" Ali asked.

"Sure."

"Your camel not act right," Ali declared. "You change to pack animal."

The rest of the caravan waited while Ali and the boys took the pack from one of the other camels and lashed it onto Bert's unruly mount. Then Bert mounted the pack camel. Finally the riders set off again across the desert.

They stopped once to eat their sandwiches and fruit and sat in the small amount of shade afforded by the kneeling camels. In the middle of the afternoon Mr. Mallakh suddenly pointed ahead. "There's our dig!" he exclaimed.

In a large hollow space surrounded by sand

dunes they could see a number of men in native dress. Some were working with pick and shovel while others trundled wheelbarrows from place to place.

When Mr. Mallakh and his party rode into the dig, a slender young man left the workers and came up to them. The archaeologist introduced him as the foreman, Yussef.

"You remember Halif, who worked for us for a while?" Mr. Mallakh asked him.

When the man nodded, Bert spoke up eagerly, "Has he been here?"

"Yes, he came yesterday. He wanted work for a few days until a business transaction went through!" The foreman looked disgusted. "I sent him away. He is a troublemaker and I do not trust him."

"We've lost him again!" Nan sighed.

"That's too bad," Mr. Mallakh said. "We'll camp here tonight and go back to Cairo tomorrow if you wish."

Bert had been watching the workmen as they went about their tasks. Suddenly he caught Mr. Mallakh's arm and said excitedly, "That workman in the blue robe over there just took something from that pile of pottery and put it up his sleeve!"

The archaeologist glanced at the workman, then began to run toward him. "Halif!" he cried. "He must have sneaked back here!"

When the man saw Mr. Mallakh approaching, he looked frightened. Quickly he turned and ran toward a group of camels tethered nearby. The next minute he had jumped onto one and began riding out into the desert at a fast pace.

"Stop him!" Ali suddenly shouted. "That my Farah he riding!"

"We could never catch him," Yussef declared. "Halif has the fastest racing camel I've ever seen."

"She *my* camel," Ali corrected him proudly. "She stolen from shed last week! I must get her back!"

"I thought you sent Halif away," Mr. Mallakh reminded his foreman.

"He must have come back last night," Yussef said. "He probably thought he could keep out of my sight until he had a chance to steal something."

By this time Halif's blue robe was only a spot in the distance against the yellow sand.

"Never mind," Mr. Mallakh said consolingly when he noticed Ali's dark eyes filled with tears. "We'll radio to the Cairo police to be on the lookout for Halif and your camel."

"Radio?" Bert asked, surprised.

The archaeologist explained that the dig maintained radio contact with the Cairo police in case of any emergency. "Yussef is our operator."

As the foreman hurried away to make the report, the children began to unload their camels. The boys set up the two tents they had brought, one for Terry and Nan and the other for Bert and Danny.

Mr. Mallakh had a small hut which he used while at the dig. Ali preferred to roll up in a blanket on the sand.

When everything had been stowed away, the three American children met outside the tents. Ali had gone over to talk to some of the workmen.

"It's too bad that Yussef sent Halif away," Bert remarked.

"But Halif didn't stay away," Nan pointed out. "He evidently wanted to get out of Cairo for a few days."

"That's right," Bert agreed. "Say, maybe he's still planning to hide somewhere!"

"Bert, he might come back here!" his twin exclaimed.

"Right. Let's search the dig," Bert proposed.

"You kids are silly!" Danny jeered. "Halif is probably a thousand miles away by this time!"

Nan and Bert paid no attention. They walked away.

Danny changed his mind. "There's nothing to do here," he said. "I may as well come."

Nan winked at Bert. They knew Danny was afraid he would miss some excitement if he did not tag along.

The children paced slowly through the excavations. Here and there they saw deep pits dug in the ground, some with ladders leading down into them.

"It's a huge place," Danny remarked as he gazed over the area which was being worked.

"This looks like a good spot to hide," said Nan. She indicated a large hole in the ground. A ladder hung over the side.

"There's a tunnel leading away from one end of the pit," Bert pointed out. "Let's go down."

One by one the children descended the crude wooden ladder to the floor of the excavation. Then with Bert in the lead they made their way along the narrow passageway. Finally it ended at a solid wall of dirt.

"I guess Halif isn't down here," Nan remarked. "We'd better go back."

They turned, with Danny taking the lead this time. When they came out of the tunnel, he cried, "Where's the ladder?"

"Why, it's gone!" Nan exclaimed.

"Maybe it fell down," Bert suggested.

Frantically they searched the bottom of the pit. The ladder was not in sight.

"What will we do?" Danny cried. He looked frightened.

"Yell!" Bert advised. Together the three children shouted at the top of their lungs. "Help! Help!" There was no reply.

Finally Nan said, "I think the desert wind is blowing the sound of our voices away from the camp. They'll never hear us."

"We'll have to signal some other way," Bert decided. "What can we use?"

Nan took the red cotton scarf from her dark hair. "Try this."

Bert took it. "You're the tallest, Danny. You stand against the side. I'll climb up on your shoulders and wave Nan's scarf."

"Oh I hope someone sees it!" Nan said.

Danny grunted when Bert planted his feet on the boy's shoulders. But he braced. himself against the pit side and stood firm. Bert held up the scarf and began to wave it from side to side. It just reached the level of the ground.

After about ten minutes a dark face peered over the side. It was Yussef!

"The ladder is gone! We're stuck down here!" Bert called to him.

Yussef disappeared, but a few seconds later the ladder was pushed over the side of the pit. Quickly the children scrambled up.

"I'd like to know who took that ladder away!" Bert said indignantly.

"I see a clue!" Nan bent down and picked up a small scrap of blue cotton clinging to the rough wood on one rung.

"Maybe whoever pulled up the ladder wore a blue galabia!" Bert cried.

"Halif!" Nan exclaimed.

"Let's tell Mr. Mallakh!" Bert urged.

The archaeologist was disturbed when he heard the children's story. "If Halif is around this camp, we'll find him!" he declared. A party of workmen was assigned to search.

When they reported that Halif was not in the dig area, Mr. Mallakh sent two men out on camels to scout the desert for the fugitive.

"It's getting cold!" Nan shivered.

"And windier!" Terry remarked, clutching her head scarf.

"This is usual for the desert," Mr. Mallakh said. "The temperature drops as much as twenty degrees at night and a strong wind often comes up at sunset."

Supper was served to the group as they sat around a campfire. Mr. Mallakh entertained the others with stories of his expeditions.

"This one is funny," he said. "I once traveled with some friends to the coast of Greece. On a certain day while we were digging for treasures, one of the men saw a round piece of gold in the dirt. He was sure it must be a very old and valuable coin and called us all to look.

"The ladder is gone! We're stuck down here!" Bert called

"He dashed over and picked it up. Well, my friend felt pretty silly. As we all gathered around, he said, 'This is only my old watch that I dropped in the dirt!' "

The children laughed, and Flossie begged for another story.

Mr. Mallakh smiled. "Here's one just for you, Flossie." All the twins and Danny listened, however.

He continued, "At home I have a prize kitten."

Instantly Danny Rugg frowned as he thought of his disappearing dinner.

"I had a terrible time," said the storyteller, "trying to find a suitable name for my kitten. Then one day a kitchen servant accidentally spilled some lemon juice on the floor. The kitten quickly licked it up."

"Oh, what's her name?" Flossie piped up eagerly.

"It ought to be Sour Puss!" Danny burst out, and everyone laughed.

"It's not, though," said Mr. Mallakh. "I call her Limona."

"That's a pretty name," said Nan.

Presently two scouts rode into camp on camels.

"Any luck?" Mr. Mallakh asked them.

"No, we not find Halif. We search again tomorrow," one of them answered.

In a little while everyone said good night and went to bed. Bert stretched out wearily in his sleeping bag. The events of the day passed through his mind, and he could not go to sleep. The boy kept wondering where Omir and Halif were, and what had happened to Uncle Abdel's servant, Salah.

Then, just as Bert was drifting off to sleep, he heard a roar. "Wind!" he told himself.

Suddenly there was a sharp snapping sound. The next instant the tent rose from the ground and sailed off across the desert!

# CHAPTER XVI

## DESERT MIRAGE

"HEY!" Bert yelled as he sat upright and saw the tent fly through the air.

The sudden gust of wind woke Danny. "What happened to the tent?" he asked in surprise.

The commotion roused Mr. Mallakh and the girls. They rushed over to the boys, who stood peering in bewilderment at the wooden stakes. This was all that remained of their shelter.

"The wind snapped the tent ropes!" Danny cried.

Mr. Mallakh stooped to examine the pegs. "That doesn't seem likely," he said doubtfully. "I don't think the wind was strong enough for that. The stakes held."

Bert crouched beside the archaeologist. The boy pointed to one of the wooden pegs. One end of the tent rope was still tied tightly around it. The other end was frayed.

"This rope has been cut almost through," the boy declared. "Someone has tampered with the ropes so a strong gust of wind would break them!"

"I'll bet it was Halif!" Nan cried. "He's trying to scare us!"

Mr. Mallakh quickly ordered the camp searched once more. There was still no sign of the thief.

"You boys bring your sleeping bags into my hut," Mr. Mallakh ordered. "We can't do anything more about finding Halif tonight."

"I wish to get Farah away from that bad man," Ali said wistfully the next morning as the group was eating breakfast.

"Perhaps we can," Mr. Mallakh answered. "Yussef thinks that Halif may have gone to an oasis some distance away from here toward the Suez Canal. If you boys and girls don't mind another long camel ride, we could go there."

"Oh, let's!" Nan urged. "I love camel riding!" The boys were enthusiastic too.

"And we *must* find Halif before Omir does," Bert reminded the others.

The archaeologist supervised the packing of a picnic lunch. "We can rest at the oasis and be back here late in the afternoon," he told Terry and the children.

It was still early in the morning as the procession started off across the desert. They all wore light hats and scarves around their necks to protect them from the hot sun.

They had ridden for about an hour when Nan stood up in her stirrups and looked around the desert. "I see a man on horseback," she said in surprise. "He looks as if he's trying to catch up with us."

Mr. Mallakh stared at the galloping horseman. "It's Yussef! Something must have happened at the dig which he wants to tell me about."

The riders reined in their camels. In a few minutes the foreman reached them. He pulled a drawing from his robe and began to question Mr. Mallakh.

The archaeologist turned to the others. "This may take a while," he said. "There's no need for you to wait. You'll be cooler riding and I'll catch up with you as soon as I finish talking to Yussef. Ali, you know the way to the oasis. Just ride straight toward the canal."

The Egyptian boy grinned. "I be guide," he promised.

The children took advantage of the stop to drink from their water canteens, then the procession plodded on.

Some time later Danny said to Bert, "I don't think Ali knows where he's going. I wish Mr.

"A mirage!" Danny yelled. "We're lost!"

Mallakh would hurry. We could be lost in this crazy desert!"

"I'm sure Ali is going the right way," Bert tried to assure Danny, but the boy looked uneasily around at the vast expanse of yellow sand.

Suddenly Ali halted his camel. "Look!" he cried. "Ship on canal!"

Terry and the children gazed toward the horizon. They could just make out the top of a ship moving slowly along. It appeared to be going through the sand.

"It's a mirage!" Danny yelled. "We're going the wrong way! We're lost! I knew it!" He wheeled his camel around and urged it into a fast lope.

"Danny! Wait!" Bert cried.

But the frightened boy paid no attention. He kicked his mount until it went even faster.

"I go after him," Ali volunteered.

"I think we should all stay together," Terry said nervously. "We'll come too!"

The riders prodded their camels into a fast pace and followed Danny. But his camel was speedy and he had a head start. They could not come close enough to reason with him.

Finally after ten minutes, Danny's camel slowed down. Ali rode up and grasped the reins.

"You never ride into desert alone," the Egyptian boy said sternly. "We not lost."

Danny looked sheepish. "Are you sure that ship wasn't a mirage?" he asked.

"Yes. She on Suez Canal. It run like big ditch across desert. Now we go back." Ali motioned the others to turn around.

After a few minutes, however, Ali began to look uneasy. "Sun straight above us," he said. "I not sure of direction!"

"Perhaps if we ride to the top of that big sand dune," Bert suggested, "you can tell us where we should go."

"Okay!" Ali agreed, and led the way to the top of the sand hill.

Terry and the children gazed out over the desert. There was nothing in sight but more dunes and unbroken stretches of yellow sand. Ali shook his head in discouragement.

"What are we going to do?" Danny asked.

"If we had some way to signal, perhaps Mr. Mallakh would see it," Nan proposed. "He must be looking for us."

Terry drew a powder compact from her pocket and opened it. "How about this?" she said, pointing to the mirror in the lid.

"Just the thing!" Bert took the mirror, held it up to catch the sun's rays and moved it back and forth. A stream of light flashed from it. The others looked eagerly around for some reply to the signal.

At last Nan cried out, "I see a flash over there to the right!"

"It must be Mr. Mallakh," Ali cried. "Let's go!"

Happily, the group rode down from the dune and headed in the direction of the flashing light. Bert continued to send his signal.

At the end of fifteen minutes the children saw Mr. Mallakh riding toward them. They waved eagerly.

"What happened to you?" he asked. "I was afraid you were lost until I saw your signal!"

Ali hung his head. "I mixed up," he said. "We lost until Bert signal!"

"It wasn't all your fault," Bert spoke up. He looked at Danny.

The boy flushed. "I guess I was mostly to blame," he confessed reluctantly. "I thought the ship Ali saw on the canal was a mirage."

Mr. Mallakh smiled. "I'm glad everything turned out all right. Shall we go on to the oasis?"

"When do we eat?" Danny whispered to Ali as the procession got under way again.

"Mr. Mallakh think it too hot to eat in sun," the Egyptian boy replied. "We near oasis now."

A short while later the children saw ahead of them a small settlement of flat-roofed mud houses. There were palm trees waving in the hot breeze and patches of green fields. Just beyond, the travelers caught a glimpse of blue water.

"The oasis is on the bank of the canal," Mr. Mallakh explained. "I think before we ride into the village we should eat our lunch." He motioned toward a green area.

"It's about time!" Danny muttered under his breath.

Gratefully the children and Terry slipped from their camels. Nan and the counselor opened the package of lunch which Ali had taken from the back of his camel.

"This tastes wonderful!" Terry remarked as she bit into a sandwich while Nan poured cold lemonade from a Thermos into paper cups.

"It sure does!" Bert sighed blissfully.

When all the food was gone, Mr. Mallakh stood up. "I think it might be a good idea to walk into the village," he suggested. "We will attract less attention that way."

The streets of the oasis were empty. The only sound was the occasional grunt of a camel or the cry of a child.

"Everyone must be asleep!" Nan said, giggling.

Ali was walking in front with Mr. Mallakh. Suddenly he gave a low, peculiar whistle. Instantly a grunting, groaning noise came from a nearby hut followed by the sound of hoofs thudding against earth.

"Farah!" Ali dashed to the door of the hut and threw it open. A camel was tied to an iron ring in the floor.

"Farah! I find you!" The Egyptian boy flung his arms around the animal's neck. Happy tears ran down his brown cheeks.

Ali quickly untied the rope and led the camel from the hut.

"Then Halif *must* be around here somewhere," Bert whispered excitedly, when they all gathered in the street again. "He wouldn't just leave Farah here for good, especially since he went to all the trouble of stealing her."

"Yes," said Ali. He beamed, still holding tightly to his prize camel. "Bad men know she very fast."

Again the group wandered down the vacant streets, hoping to find someone who could give them information about Halif. Finally they spotted a man stretching sleepily in his doorway.

Mr. Mallakh suggested that Ali describe Halif to him and ask if the thief were in the village. They approached and soon Ali was in rapid conversation with him in Arabic. Finally the boy turned to the others.

"Man show us hut Halif use here!" he told them.

After exchanging excited glances, the searchers fell in behind their guide. He took them to the outskirts of town and pointed out a two-room hut. Bert beckoned to the group to follow him quietly up to it. He went to a window and peeked in.

"It's empty!" he exclaimed.

The twins and Danny ran around the side and went in the door. They hoped to find some clues about where Halif had gone.

"Wait a minute," Bert said. "Do you hear something?"

The others listened intently. "Someone's in the next room!" Nan cried. "It sounds as if he's trying to call out."

"Halif! He must be in there," Danny said. "We'd better watch our step."

"Oh, come on!" Bert urged. "Let's see."

The two boys walked softly to the closed door. Bert pulled it open.

"Oh!" Nan gasped.

A man in Egyptian robes lay face down in one corner. He was tightly bound!

# CHAPTER XVII

### SALAH'S STORY

"HALIF!" Bert ran to the man and turned him over. "It's not Halif!" he cried then. "This is Salah!"

With Ali's help he quickly untied the rope which bound the man. Salah stretched and rose unsteadily to his feet.

"How did you get here?" Nan burst out.

The man's face grew red with rage. "That scoundrel Halif!" he cried. "He tricked me and stole my master's treasure!"

Bert and Danny led the still shaking man out of the hut and helped him to a seat under a tree.

"Where is Halif now?" Bert asked.

"Probably in Cairo." In reply to the children's questions, the man told them that Halif had come to the oasis very late the night before but had left early that morning. Halif had boasted that he had bought a racing camel from a Damascus man named Omir.

"He left the camel near here for safekeeping, but I don't know where," Salah said.

"The camel belongs to our friend, Ali," Bert remarked. "And we found it on the way here."

"But tell us how Halif got the toy horse," Terry urged.

Again Salah's face darkened. "Halif stopped me when I left Mr. Mallakh's house with the horse," he began. "He told me Mr. Gouda wished me to deliver the package to him at the museum. I know my master often gives things to the museum. Halif once worked for him so I went to the museum with that thief."

Salah struck his forehead with his palm. "I am stupid!" he cried.

"What happened at the museum?" Nan urged him to continue.

Salah said that when he and Halif had arrived at the museum, an attendant had told them Mr. Gouda had been called to the dig. He wished Salah to bring the antique horse to him there.

"Halif said he would go along and he got camels for the trip."

"So it *was* you I saw with Halif at the museum!" Bert exclaimed. "Go on."

"A short distance out in the desert Halif was met by a friend of his," the servant continued.

"The two of them forced me to come here to the oasis with them. When Halif went away, the other man stayed here and kept me prisoner. Then Halif came back, and this morning they bound me and left me alone. I tried to loosen the ropes but could not."

Salah buried his head in his arms. "Oh, what will my master do to me?" he wailed.

"You'll have to help us recover the horse," Bert declared. "Have you any idea where Halif lives in Cairo?"

"I think he lives in the aqueduct in Old Cairo," Salah said.

"Lives in an aqueduct?" Terry repeated in amazement. "How could that be?"

Mr. Mallakh explained that some of the poor people of Cairo had built themselves shacks under the arches of the ancient aqueduct. "This wall was constructed almost eight hundred years ago to carry water to the Citadel."

"We must go back to Cairo right now!" Bert declared. "Halif may sell the horse to someone else!"

"He has two customers for it," Salah said. "Halif boasted to his friend that he could sell the antique either to a shop owner in Damascus or to the president of a perfume factory in Cairo."

"He didn't sell it to Mr. Attiyah in Damascus," Nan pointed out, "so he must be taking it to the perfume man."

But which perfume man?" Bert asked. "There must be more than one in Cairo!"

"He is man who have shop across from museum. My father say he collector," Ali said.

"Come on!" Bert said impatiently. "We'd better get going!"

Ali happily climbed up on Farah while Salah took the camel the boy had ridden from the dig.

"We won't be able to get to Cairo until tomorrow," Bert fumed, "and by that time Halif may have sold the toy horse!"

"You'll never find that horse!" Danny predicted.

"I think I can help you," Mr. Mallakh remarked. "When we get back to the dig I'll radio for the police helicopter to come out from Cairo and pick you up."

"That's wonderful!" Nan exclaimed. "Then we'll be in the city by evening."

As they rode toward the dig, the children discussed the mystery. They decided that Halif had probably spied on Mr. Mallakh. He also knew that Mr. Gouda had purchased the valuable antique and would send Salah to pick it up.

"That museum attendant must have been in on the plot too," Nan surmised, "since he gave out the message to go to the dig."

"But why didn't Halif pretend to take Salah to the dig in the first place?" Danny asked.

Bert spoke in a low voice. "I think he was trying to confuse Salah so he wouldn't suspect anything. Remember, Uncle Abdel said Salah isn't too bright."

Because of their eagerness to return to Cairo, the children and Terry urged their camels to a faster pace. They reached the dig in a shorter time than it had taken them to reach the oasis.

Mr. Mallakh immediately put in a radio call to the Cairo mamour. "They'll send a helicopter right out," he reported a few minutes later.

In less than an hour they heard the whir of the helicopter, and watched it settle down on a strip of sand.

"It looks pretty small," Terry observed. "I don't believe it can take all of us."

She was right. When the pilot hurried up to speak to Mr. Mallakh, he looked surprised to see the four children and Terry.

"My 'copter will hold only three," he said. "Which ones want to go with me?"

Ali answered. "Bert and Nan go. They work most on mystery." He grinned. "I ride Farah. No fly!"

Terry and Mr. Mallakh agreed to this proposal. They would ride camels to Cairo with Danny and Salah the next morning.

"Catch Halif!" said Ali as the Bobbseys boarded the helicopter.

"See you tomorrow," Bert and Nan called as

"Catch Halif!" Ali said to the Bobbseys

the pilot closed the door. A few seconds later the helicopter rose into the air and turned toward the city.

When the craft came down at the police airfield, the children found Tom waiting for them with one of Uncle Abdel's cars.

"How did you know we were coming?" Nan asked in amazement.

"The mamour telephoned the house and told us you were on your way," the counselor explained. "He says you think you have a clue to the theft of the antique horse. The police haven't been able to find it, so they're going to let you follow any leads you have. They'll stand by to give you help if you need it."

"That's great!" Bert declared. "The first thing we want to do is go to the perfume shop across from the museum. We think Halif may have sold the horse to the owner."

"Okay," Tom agreed. "Hop in the car and we'll be on our way!"

During the drive into town Bert and Nan told the story of their adventures at the dig.

"You kids really are great detectives," Tom declared. He drove up before a shop displaying many bottles of perfume in the small window. "Is this the place you mean?" he asked.

"Yes."

Tom parked the car and walked into the shop

with the twins. The room was small and was lined with glass cases filled with bottles of all sizes.

A dark-haired young man came toward the visitors. "Good evening," he said. "May I help you? You are interested in some nice perfumes?"

Bert spoke up. "Are you the owner of this shop, sir?"

The young man smiled. "No. I'm sorry. The owner has been out of town for several days and has not yet returned."

"Oh dear!" Nan sounded disappointed. She turned to the others. "What shall we do now?"

"Perhaps there is something I can do for you?" the clerk suggested.

"Actually we're looking for a man named Halif," Bert explained. "Do you know him?"

The clerk seemed puzzled for a moment, then his face brightened. "I believe that is the man who was in here earlier today. He too was looking for my employer."

"Did he leave a message or say where he could be reached?" Nan asked eagerly.

The clerk walked to the rear of the shop and took a slip of paper from a desk. "The man left this address and suggested the owner meet him there."

Bert and Nan exchanged triumphant glances.

"May we see that address?" Bert requested.

The clerk looked hesitant but passed it to Bert. The boy examined the paper, then turned to Nan.

"I'm sure this is what we're looking for!" he cried.

## CHAPTER XVIII

### HORSE! HURRAH!

AFTER Nan looked at the paper, she showed it to Tom. On the slip was a crude drawing of the aqueduct. An arrow pointed to one of the shacks.

"This must be Halif's home!" she exclaimed.

"It sure is," said Bert. "Come on! We've got him this time!"

With the paper clutched in his hand, he ran toward the front door of the shop. The clerk looked bewildered.

"Wait a minute!" Tom advised. "I think you should call the mamour and tell him where we're going. He can send some men to make the arrest."

"I guess you're right," Bert admitted. "May I use your phone?" he asked the clerk.

When permission was given, Bert quickly

made the call. "They'll meet us at the aqueduct," he reported.

"I'm going to phone Freddie and Flossie," Nan declared. "They'll want to know what's happening."

When she finished the call, Nan joined the others. "Tom," she said, "would you mind stopping at Uncle Abdel's house to pick up Freddie and Flossie? They insist they have to be with us when we catch Halif!"

Bert grinned. "It wouldn't be fair to leave them out," he agreed.

The small twins were waiting at the curb when Tom drove up to the house.

"Isn't this 'citing?" Flossie asked as she settled herself in the front seat with Nan and Tom.

"I'm glad Ali found Farah," Freddie said. "Do you think he'll let me ride her some time?"

Bert smiled at his younger brother. "Yes. Ali is bringing her to Cairo tomorrow."

A short drive brought the group to the section of the city known as Old Cairo and they got out.

"Look!" Flossie said.

She pointed to several Egyptian boys and girls who were dancing in a circle. An old man was playing a tune for them on a long black pipe.

"That's called a *mizmaar*," Tom explained. "It's supposed to ward off evil spirits."

"We sure could use one of those now," Bert said, grinning.

"Aren't the children cute?" Flossie put in. "I like the girls' long black dresses."

"Looks like a costume party," Freddie remarked, "those blue and white striped suits the boys are wearing."

The little twins went to join the group, which seemed happy to have them. *"Keef halak?"* said one.

"How are *you?*" Flossie answered.

When the dance was over, Freddie decided to say good-by in Arabic. *"Khatrak!"* he said.

The Egyptian children looked surprised, but grinned and said, *"Khatrak!"*

Freddie and Flossie returned to their group and they walked forward. Ahead was the ancient aqueduct that looked like an arched bridge. On top was the huge trough through which water used to run in olden days. Below, the arched sections had been filled in recent years with dilapidated shacks.

"Which one is Halif's?" Nan asked.

Bert consulted the drawing, then studied the aqueduct. "It seems to me it's that one in the second story."

"But how can he get up to his house?" Flossie asked, puzzled.

"He climbs the ladder." Freddie pointed out a crude ladder which led to the upper doorway.

"Shall we go up?" Nan asked.

"I think you should wait for the police," Tom replied. "We'll park at the corner here. You can watch the place to make sure Halif doesn't leave —that is, if he's in there."

The counselor had just turned off the car motor when Freddie grabbed Bert's arm. "Someone's coming," he cried.

Two men in native dress and kuffiyahs approached the ladder. They seemed to consult each other, then began climbing to the open door above.

"Omir and Attiyah!" Bert hissed. "I recognized them when they turned this way."

"Maybe we can hear what they say." Nan slipped from the car and ran toward the aqueduct with Bert close behind her.

When the younger twins started to follow, Tom motioned them to stay by the car. "Wait for the police," he ordered. "I don't want you to get into any trouble."

"I wish the police would hurry!" Nan whispered to Bert when they reached the ladder. "I'm afraid Halif will give the horse to Omir, and he and Attiyah will get away!"

"We'll stop them somehow, Sis," Bert said firmly.

At that moment a loud burst of Arabic came from the upper shack. There were three voices of men who seemed to be having a violent argument.

"If Ali only were here," Nan said, "he could tell us what they're saying!"

She had just finished speaking when the figures of Omir and Attiyah appeared in the doorway above the twins. Halif stood behind them. They were still arguing.

"We can't let them get away!" Bert whispered. "Grab the ladder, Nan. We'll have to pull it down!"

Desperately the twins tugged at the heavy ladder. Omir was about to step onto it when it fell with a *bang!* He jumped back just in time to keep from pitching to the street.

The three men crowded in the doorway and peered down at the ground. When they saw Bert and Nan, they yelled with rage and shook their fists.

At that moment a car with four policemen whizzed up to the aqueduct. They jumped out and ran toward Bert and Nan. "Are these the thieves?" the officer in charge asked.

Bert nodded. Two of the policemen replaced the ladder and hurried up it. The twins followed.

Bert pointed to Halif. "He's the one who has Mr. Gouda's antique horse," he declared.

The man glared when the officer picked up an

object from a shelf over the bed. It was a small, brightly painted clay horse.

"That must be it!" Nan cried. "Mr. Gouda says it's one of the earliest horse figures ever to be found, and that's why it's so very valuable."

"Mr. Gouda bought it from Mr. Mallakh and is giving it to our town museum in the United States," Bert added.

"Who are these other two men?" the officer asked, indicating Omir and Attiyah.

Bert told him that Attiyah had sent Omir from Damascus to buy the stolen toy from Halif. "And we're sure Omir stole Ali's pet camel because he's wearing the brass tassel Ali made for Farah."

"He was in Mr. Gouda's house the other night trying to steal some of his collection," Nan spoke up.

Under questioning by the policeman, Omir admitted to stealing the racing camel and selling it to Halif. He had seen the Bobbseys in the pyramid and again at Pompey's Column in Alexandria. Omir realized they thought he had the toy horse and were following him.

Omir continued the confession. "A sailor friend hid me on his ship. I got into the Bobbsey boy's cabin and put a warning on his suitcase. I did this so he wouldn't be allowed to land.

"But it didn't work. The children followed me all the way to Damascus. I think they were

"We can't let them get away!" Bert whispered

as surprised as I was when the antique horse wasn't in the stuffed camel."

Omir glared at Halif. "You double-crosser! See what trouble you've got us into now!"

Halif sneered. "You didn't offer me enough money so I only pretended the horse was in the stuffed camel."

"We will go to the police station," the officer ordered. "You can tell your stories to the mamour." The officer motioned the three thieves to descend the ladder.

When everyone was back on the street, Bert asked Halif, "Why did you go out to the dig?"

"My other customer for the horse, the perfume man, was out of town and I decided to stay away from Cairo until he returned. I was afraid Omir and Attiyah might come to Cairo and force me to sell the antique to them. I was sure the perfume man would pay more."

"I'll bet you were surprised, Attiyah, when your plane took off without you," Freddie put in. Attiyah did not answer.

Omir slipped the brass tassel from his wrist. "Give this back to the boy," he said. "He's done a good job in training his camel."

"Mr. Gouda can claim his property at headquarters," the policeman told Bert just before the prisoners were driven away.

Uncle Abdel was waiting for his guests when

they finally drove home. He was happy to know that the antique horse was safe.

"Won't Terry and Ali be s'prised!" Flossie exclaimed.

Freddie agreed and added suddenly, "Boy, I'm hungry as a camel!"

"The cook has supper ready," Uncle Abdel remarked.

"Goody!" said Flossie.

It was early afternoon of the next day before Terry and the other children reached Uncle Abdel's house. All were eager to learn what had happened the night before. After hearing the story, even Danny Rugg admitted the Bobbseys had done a good job in recovering the stolen antique.

"And now that it is found, we'll have to be on our way back to Venice to rejoin the rest of our tour," Tom reminded the children.

"I don't want to leave!" Flossie declared. "I like Egypt."

Uncle Abdel had come into the room in time to hear Flossie's remark. He ruffled her yellow curls. "And Egypt likes you," he assured her. "I have just come from police headquarters. The mamour gave me the antique horse and asked me to congratulate the American children for solving the mystery of its disappearance."

He showed them the tiny toy horse. At once

Nan said, "How perfect! And to think it was made so many years ago!"

"We'll have to take very good care of it going home," Terry remarked.

The day before the Americans were to leave Cairo, Uncle Abdel told them he had planned a surprise for them.

"I love s'prises," said Flossie. "What is it?"

Mr. Gouda laughed. "I will tell you only half of it. Salah is cooking a special dinner for us."

Nan smiled. "Are we having guests?"

"You will see. Watch outside."

At dinnertime the children gathered in front of the house. "Oh, I know who it is!" Bert cried. "Here comes Ali riding Farah!"

"Hurray!" Freddie shouted. "Now we can all have a ride!"

Ali rode up grinning, and he did give each of the American boys and girls a ride up and down the street. Then he stabled the camel on Uncle Abdel's property.

Danny was chuckling. "Wait until the guys in Lakeport hear I rode a racing camel!"

"And me too!" said Freddie.

Ali took a sack from the saddle bag and led the way into the house. "Mr. Gouda say I have dinner here. I bring presents."

When dinner was over and everyone had praised Salah's good cooking, Ali slipped from his chair and ran from the room. He returned with the sack from which he took little packages. He distributed them to Mr. Gouda, Tom, Terry, and the Lakeport children.

"My father make them for you," Ali announced proudly, "because you my friends."

Eagerly everyone opened the gifts. "How darling!" Nan exclaimed.

"Mine's bee-yoo-ti-ful!" Flossie cried.

In each box lay a small brass camel with an intricately carved saddle and a tiny tassel swinging from its head! They could be used on a desk or could be worn. Everyone thanked Ali, then Freddie got up and pretended to ride around the room on the brass Farah. As everyone laughed, he called out, "I'm a camel cowboy! Yippee! Ali!"

The other twins joined in. "Yippee Ali! Yippee Cairo! Yippee Uncle Abdel!"